I0544524

Portals

By David Farrell

Also By David Farrell

The Last Resort

The Glove

You Can't Get Rid of Me That Easily

Twelve

Dropping the Belt

Twelve More

Printed in Australia
First Printing 2020

Paperback ISBN   9781647133221

For my Wife.

The adventure continues.

CHAPTER ONE

Maree watched as the green line of light approached her face. From behind the glass she felt unable to move as it maintained its steady path. She flailed and pressed her palms against the invisible barrier. No sound had escaped Maree's mouth. The rumbling electrical hum became louder as she shook from side to side and her hair flew in front of her face. Suddenly the beam was upon her, and it scanned painlessly from her left side to her right. As the light penetrated her eyes Maree froze and clenched them shut.

She sat up and gasped in the cool night air. Her dream of being trapped inside a photocopier had been so vivid that Maree instinctively looked around the room to double-check that she'd actually escaped it. Lying next to her was Maree's husband Leon, who'd slept blissfully through her anxiety. She studied his stubbled face for a sign that he might be faking it, that he'd actually woken up, but he remained placid and unmoving. Maree sipped from a glass of water by her bedside table.

4.27am

Was there any point going back to sleep? She wondered. Maree feared that if her mind found itself capable of dreaming that she would once again be tormented with a similar nightmare. *But why was she dreaming about photocopiers?* Visions of her workplace had never manifested themselves subconsciously before. Now that she was the sole breadwinner Maree decided that perhaps there was an unspoken pressure upon her. She was now fearful about losing her job. The idea of both her and Leon being unemployed would paint them as failures. They'd already lost their house, being forced to leave the property market almost as soon as they'd entered it. Now that they were living in her parent's spare room one could argue that the damage had been done. Maree wished she felt less anxious about the future.

Leon had started snoring. His eyelids flickered slightly as he exhaled deeply. Maree wondered what he was dreaming about. He looked so peaceful. Maree's mind was now racing, and she determined that sleep would be impossible. She crept out of the bed and into the en suite before turning on a light.

She examined her pale face in front of the mirror. There were bags forming underneath her green-brown eyes. Maree brushed out her messy brown hair and started to clean her teeth. Ever since she was a teenager she'd always had a strict oral hygiene regimen. Maree brushed three times a day; once as soon as she woke up, again after a late breakfast as well as at the end of the night. It was an obsessive habit that Maree had formed after watching a video about tooth decay. She'd never forgotten the horrible imagery. One added benefit had been the complete elimination of morning breath. When they'd first started dating Leon had been amazed at how great her breath was first thing in the morning. These days their kisses were a lot less frequent.

Maree drove to work early that morning without disturbing her husband or her sleeping parents. She had no idea how late Leon had been up working on his novel the night before. She kept waiting to hear how it had progressed, or for an invitation to read some. Her husband slept in often, and the two were starting to live separate lives. Leon had stopped shaving and had taken to wearing sweatpants. He was becoming more and more antisocial. He didn't like to leave their bedroom without Maree, making her feel like a go-between, couriering messages from her parents to Leon and back again. She knew why he didn't want to face them. Leon still felt embarrassed. He had vowed to provide for her, a promise that he'd made to Maree on their wedding day, and now Leon was feeling worthless. She wasn't sure how to proceed.

Maree wanted her husband to find a job so they could move out again and salvage their relationship. Without employment she didn't know how much longer they could stay in this living arrangement. Maree felt powerless and to distract herself she opted to blast the radio on her way to the office.

Being early had its advantages as Maree slid into the parking spot closest to the door. The office building was located in the northern suburbs of Melbourne, which had become a very trendy area. Maree loved the idea of living within walking distance to Carlton Gardens. On the nicer Melbourne days she liked to walk to the fountain and back, eating a homemade sandwich as she basked in the sunlight, and people-watched the locals. On rainy days eight hours in an office sometimes felt like ten.

She recognised her supervisor Lachlan's car parked opposite her own. Maree wondered what unholy hour he'd arrived.

***

There was always something to photocopy at Channel Four, which may have been the inspiration for her recent nightmares. In her twenties Maree had worked in places where saving the environment meant something, and printing and copying was done sparingly. Here the photocopier was suffering from overuse. Maree was a part of a sales team that sold commercial television airtime to clients. She found it dull, as did most of the employees at Channel Four. Lachlan insisted on keeping physical files on everything, fearing either an audit or a cyber attack. It meant that Maree was out of her chair regularly. This workload had led her to bond with Marcus. With his blonde hair and easy smile, he was undoubtedly her work crush. His desk was conveniently located next to the printer, resulting in many flirtatious interactions and shared moments throughout her day. It felt like Maree was in one long conversation that they just paused from time to time, always picking it up again seamlessly. They had a rhythm that she found difficult to ignore.

'Are you wearing two matching anklets?' asked Marcus, indicating toward her feet, 'or are those gold chains part of the top of your shoes?'

'I'm wearing two anklets, but they don't match,' replied Maree.

'Oh… that's cool.'

'You're very observant, aren't you?' she said, wondering why he'd been staring at her feet with such interest.

'Only when there's someone around worth observing,' Marcus responded, as he flashed Maree a trademark smile.

She'd discovered last year that they'd both previously kept the same breed of dog: a border collie. One thing in common had led to another and now she timed her walks to the kitchen to coincide with his. She liked being left alone with him. Maree watched as Marcus filled up a light blue drink bottle that was almost the same colour as his eyes.

'Are you ready for my question of the day?' asked Marcus, screwing on the lid of his bottle and giving his ear lobe a quick scratch. This had become the latest in a string of reasons for them to interact.

'I don't know, is it a good one? Would you say it's the *best* question yet?' asked Maree with a smile.

'That's like asking a father to choose his favourite child! I couldn't possibly say if it's the best,' he stated, moving out of the way of the tap.

'You don't have any children.'

'That I know of! But someday I'd love to have a family.'

Maree smiled and started to fill her own drink bottle. Only the lid appeared metal, while the body of the container featured a faux bamboo sticker.

'You'd better get started soon. You're not getting any younger,' she said. Flirting with Marcus was so easy.

'Noted,' he said. 'Now, which superpower would you rather have…'

'Really? Superpowers?' she asked, interrupting his line of questioning.

'Hear me out! Would you rather be able to fly or turn invisible?'

Maree paused for a moment while she considered the options.

'Oh gosh. Would I be able to carry another person when I'm flying around?'

'No. You don't have super strength! Just the ability to fly,' replied Marcus.

'So… if I go and fly away on a holiday I can't bring anyone with me?'

'You can… but they'd have to meet you there I guess.'

'If I were invisible I'd probably see a lot of things I didn't want to see,' reasoned Maree.

'There is always that risk.'

'I don't know. It's like one is a way of escaping where you're gone physically, you've flown away, and the other is like everyone thinks you're gone but they just can't see you,' she said. 'You're still there but they don't know it.'

'I suppose so.'

'Sometimes I feel like I'm invisible already,' confessed Maree.

Marcus leaned in closer and Maree felt herself filling with nerves. Their drink bottles accidently clinked together. She stood her ground, allowing a rush of adrenaline to move through her.

'I'd like to think I see you Maree,' he said.

It was simple, but it was more complimentary than her husband Leon had been in weeks.

'Thanks Marcus.'

***

The office was intentionally bland. The beaten-down employees were discouraged from bringing in personal items, which meant the only pops of personality were on their computer screens. This was why Maree loved Candice. Today she'd brightened the dull office environment with a rainbow-coloured shirt and leg warmers that she wore on her wrists. None of the other twenty employees had made an effort, and Maree noted that all of the men were wearing shirts she'd seen before. Candice couldn't disappear in a crowd if she'd wanted to. Maree's best friend was tall and blonde. In her spare time she dabbled in the world of modelling. Their mutual distain for their current careers had tightened the friendship, and Maree looked forward to being around Candice on days like today. The windows were inconveniently high, making them impossible to look out of while seated. The clicking of keyboards and the low rumble of air conditioning created the feeling of a tomb. Many of the sales team had been there for over a decade, waiting for something better or for the promise of a juicy redundancy. The management team knew this and so there existed a constant stalemate, each party hoping the other would give up first. Candice approached Maree's desk and opened up a fashion magazine to reveal a familiar face.

'Ugh. Looks like Monica went to Paris again. I hate her,' said Candice.

'Wow. She looks great,' replied Maree. Monica and Candice had competed in the same modelling circles as amateurs, before the former went pro.

'I've got to lose some weight so they take me seriously in time for fashion week.'

'You look fine.'

'Just fine?' asked Candice.

'Better than fine. You look hot,' Maree responded reassuringly. She would've loved to look half as glamorous as Candice did on that Monday.

'Not as hot as Monica.' Candice was aggravated. Maree knew it must have been difficult to watch from the sidelines as someone else lived the life you wanted.

'Beauty is in the eye of the beholder.'

Candice shrugged and scooped up the magazine. She parked herself on the edge of Maree's desk and continued to flip through the pages. Maree became aware of Marcus on the other side of the room. The two had always faced each other, and on this occasion Marcus was watching her, his blue eyes admiring Maree. She could tell he was staring but she didn't mind. Maree smiled at him, and he smiled back. Candice nudged her, waking her from the daydream.

'Someone catching your eye there, beholder?' she said playfully.

'Stop it!'

Maree hadn't needed to tell Candice about her secret crush. She'd worked it out all by herself. Maree knew nothing could happen, but it didn't stop her from wondering what it would be like to be with Marcus. She and Leon had gotten married in Las Vegas on a whim during their first year together. Now life was sucking all of the romance away from their fairy tale love story. Dinners and intimate nights together had evolved into mismatched schedules, snoring and washing old underwear. The fantasy of starting again with someone new like Marcus was intriguing, but Maree worried that if she actually took that leap that it would just end up the same way. Everyone had underwear, and underwear got old. Maree didn't want to live in a boring domestic world like the one she now shared with Leon. She felt guilty for even considering ending things with her husband, as they now lived with her parents. Where would he go if she kicked him to the kerb now? His mother lived on the other side of the world and Leon's father had died years ago. Maree had become something of a surrogate parent to him, supporting his new writing dream and picking up after him like a maid. The transition had only hurt their marriage.

'Somebody likes you…' whispered Candice. Maree tried not to look in Marcus' direction, even though she could feel him watching her. It was exciting to feel wanted.

'I have work to do!' she said in a singsong voice. It didn't stop Candice from continuing to make her feel uncomfortable.

'Maree and Marcus sitting in a tree, K-I-S-S-I-N-G…' Candice was speaking too loudly, drawing the attention of several nearby employees. Maree tried to ignore her. Candice seemed to become bored with the teasing and went back to her magazine. While Maree was looking at her computer screen an email from Marcus popped up.

You look nice today.

Maree smiled. She didn't think she looked particularly nice, having rushed out the door without giving her appearance too much thought. She replied to the email and noticed out of the corner of her eye that Marcus was smiling at her.

It's hair-washing night tonight!

She discreetly watched him receive and read her words. There was something so likeable about the way he carried himself. Maree watched the corner of his mouth curl as he typed her a reply.

You'd never know!

Candice made an audible groan that made Maree quickly minimise her email.

'You want a coffee? I need to go for a walk,' stated Candice, as she stood up.

'Only if you're getting one,' answered Maree.

'Nah, I'm bitter enough.'

Lachlan, the office manager, came out of his office holding a laptop in his hands. His perfectly styled hair was held together with gel, and his suit looked impossibly crisp. Maree knew that this man had no life outside of this place. It wasn't just that he had arrived earlier than her; he just never seemed to have anything else to talk about besides sales targets. Lachlan scanned the room and then yelled out, addressing the group.

'Is anyone else having performance issues?' he called.

Candice bit her lip, which almost set off Maree.

'Anyone?'

The room was silent.

'So, I'm the only one experiencing performance issues today?' Lachlan asked again.

'Sounds like it,' replied Candice.

Lachlan was oblivious to the double entendre of his words. He closed the laptop and paced through the workplace, ignoring Candice and Maree, his eyes landing on Tim.

'Tim!' exclaimed Lachlan with an authoritative boom.

'Yes boss,' he replied, straightening his glasses as he sat upright in his chair.

'Tim! Tell me what you've been working on today?'

'Today?'

'Yes Tim. Have you succeeded in making any profitable sales at all today?' asked Lachlan.

'I have been on the phone all morning...' Tim replied, his voice trailing away.

'With who? Because I've been reviewing your work and it isn't good.'

'It's not?'

This style of management was Lachlan's bread and butter. He would isolate a weaker member of the team and publicly ridicule their efforts. Lachlan had always been more stick than carrot.

'I have been struggling to even refer to it as *work* Tim.'

Lachlan continued to use his name, which seemed to be part of the routine. Tim stammered some words, but Lachlan proceeded to berate him.

'To be honest I'm at a loss with you. Your numbers have been abysmal,' stated Lachlan.

Maree couldn't stand to watch anymore. She didn't like Lachlan's obvious abuse of power and the way he seemed to revel in it. She skimmed some papers on her desk and selected one that she'd printed that morning. Maree carried it over and placed it on Tim's desk.

'Sorry to interrupt,' she began, 'but I think you left this on the printer Tim. Looks like you snagged a pretty big sale there. Congrats!'

Maree raised an eyebrow encouragingly, out of sight of their boss. Tim caught on quickly and seemed appreciative that she was saving him from this embarrassment.

'Oh… yeah… thanks Maree.'

'Let me see that,' grumbled Lachlan as he took the paper from Tim's hands. The room was quiet again as their manager looked at the paper, absorbing the information on it. Tim waited nervously. A look of calm fell over Lachlan and he handed the paper back.

'It seems I might have misjudged you Tim. Carry on,' said Lachlan, and he returned to his office.

Maree gave Tim a pat on the back and wandered back to her desk. It was worth it to sacrifice her sale for Tim, who always tried so hard. Marcus had an approving grin on his face. Maree pretended not to notice him watching her from across the room as she sat back down.

***

As she pulled into the driveway of her parents house Maree tried to be positive. She grabbed her bag and headed into the ageing three-bedroom home. The outside of the house had started to become unkempt, as her stepfather Bill had lost interest in gardening in favour of cooking. There had been some early conversations from her mother Val about Leon helping with the yard that had never eventuated. In the living room was an all too familiar sight. Val and Bill sat in large matching chairs. Both were retired and very comfortably reclined. Their marriage seemed so easy to Maree. They didn't need anything from one another, happily seated side by side. This was a relationship that worked. Val brought her half-moon reading glasses up to her eyes to look at the back of a puzzle box. Maree assumed that her mother must have finished the previous puzzle that she'd been working on. In retirement there seemed to be lots of time for frivolity.

'Hi sweetheart. How was work?' asked Val, without looking up from the box.

'Good thanks Mum. How are you two doing?'

'Another day in paradise Maree,' replied Bill with a toothy smile. 'You should try it some time.'

'The only way I'll be retiring at age thirty is if I win the lotto.'

'Well you've got to be in it to win it!' exclaimed Bill, who'd been known to gamble from time to time.

Bill was stocky and had lost most of his hair, although Val still looked at him as though he were twenty-five. Maree's biological father George had run off with his secretary when she was only a child. She'd never been able to get all the details from her mother, who'd consistently reported that he had been *too immature* for fatherhood. After he'd left Val found her way into the arms of Bill. The two had been married since Maree was ten years old. Bill was so jovial and nice to her that she'd started thinking of him as a father from early on.

'Has Leon been down?' she asked.

'Haven't seen him,' Bill replied as he raised both eyebrows.

'We've heard him though. Bumping around up there,' added Val.

'Alright, thanks.' Maree started to head towards the stairs when Val stopped her.

'Would you remind your husband that I'd like my spare room back?'

'I'll get him onto it,' said Maree.

When they'd moved in with her parents, they'd brought a heap of furniture with them. After their wedding Maree and Leon had intended to set up their forever home and began furnishing it accordingly. When things took a financial turn for the worse they couldn't bear to part with the items. Leon had placed most of them into Val and Bill's spare room temporarily. Val had always brought up this nuisance due to the fact that Leon had never asked, rather just stored everything there assuming it would be fine. Her mother had never confronted Leon about it, rather just casually mentioned it to Maree from time to time. It was becoming a source of stress. Maree had sold most of their nicer pieces now, and the items that remained were due to be sent to the tip, at Leon's earliest convenience.

'If you two want dinner it's in the oven,' stated Val.

'Thanks Mum I'll let you know.'

At the top of the staircase Maree poked her head into the spare room. Piled up against two of the walls was the life she'd been building with Leon. The stuff was definitely clogging up an otherwise usable space. Maree caught sight of herself in the rounded mirror of a dressing table that faced the door. She looked so tired.

Leon had parked himself in a beanbag, which made his posture seem worse than it was. Her husband was now thirty-four years old, yet he was so engrossed in the video game before him that he seemed much more immature. Maree paused in the doorway for a moment, but he didn't look up. Leon's dark hair was unkempt, and his new beard made him look like a vagrant. Without a job he was unfocussed, stabbing at the buttons of his controller violently.

'Hi honey,' she said, noticing more flecks of grey in his beard. Since he'd started growing it out the grey had become more prominent.

'Hey Maree.'

She didn't like the way Leon said her name. It sounded wrong coming out of his mouth. In the past he'd always called her by a nickname, like *babe* or *sugar*. This seemed too formal. Her childhood room felt too small to accommodate them both. They'd piled up a series of boxes against the wall, which made it appear even smaller. Maree didn't want to unpack, as they'd never planned on staying.

'How's it going?' she asked.

'Good. How was your day?'

'Busy.'

Leon made a noise as he reacted to the video game, but failed to ask her why it was busy, or take any further interest. Maree gave her husband a kiss on the side of the head, but Leon was too interested in the screen in front of him to acknowledge her attempt at affection.

'Did you get much writing done today?' asked Maree.

'Uh, yeah. The creative juices have been flowing,' he replied, before mashing the buttons again.

'Great. So, is it getting close to… finished?'

'Well, I dunno, you know?'

Maree wasn't sure she did know.

'Okay… Mum's made dinner, do you want to come down and eat?'

'Ah, not really. I'm not hungry,' Leon replied.

Maree clocked a pizza box to the left of the beanbag. There were three slices remaining.

'Sure. So at work Candice told me her friend Monica is going to Paris,' said Maree, trying to engage her husband.

'Which one is Monica?'

'She's a model, you don't know her, but she's becoming really famous,' replied Maree. 'She was in this fashion magazine and…'

'Candice is the blonde, right?'

'Yeah.'

Even though he was answering her questions Leon's eyes remained glued to the screen, distracted by the outlaw character he was controlling. Maree had never really played video games and didn't understand the appeal of them.

'She looks like a model,' stated Leon matter-of-factly.

'Yeah she wants to be but these agents are really picky and-'

'Who cares about fame anyway?' said Leon, interrupting her. 'The whole fashion industry is bullshit.'

For a moment Maree wondered why her husband wanted to play with that plastic controller and not with her. She felt cast aside and manoeuvred herself around Leon in order to grab a slice of pizza. While she was enjoying her first small mouthful of the cold food Leon quickly grabbed the second last slice and placed it in his mouth to hold while he continued to play his game.

CHAPTER TWO

The man behind the wheel was about forty years old. The vehicle he was occupying was almost as old as him, but he couldn't afford to replace it. He'd driven down the vacant suburban street a little too quickly. Running on adrenaline he sipped a soda that he'd purchased with a fast food meal twenty minutes ago. The man started drifting to the left side of the road as his eyelids became heavy. Suddenly he jerked upright and slapped his cheeks, and course corrected his car back into its rightful lane. A few minutes later he was at it again, this time careening into a mailbox that shocked him back into consciousness. He blasted the radio, deciding that the noise would keep him awake and ensure he got home. He spotted a loose French fry on the passenger seat and reached for it, taking his eyes off the road momentarily.

In that instant, it appeared.

When the man looked ahead of him, he found himself on a collision course with a glowing green portal. It was large, big enough to swallow the car whole. He screamed and tried to swerve but he was going too fast and his reactions were too slow. The vehicle plunged through the portal and disappeared. The street was quiet once more.

***

There was a beam of sunlight hitting Maree in the face. She couldn't ignore it. Her husband was somehow in the shade, sleeping obliviously. She shuffled up into a sitting position and wondered whether he was actually asleep or just ignoring her.

'You awake?' she asked, trained on his face for a reaction.

Leon didn't move.

It was still early and she considered sneaking away again. Maree peeled the blankets away from herself and placed both feet on the floor. She stood and took only two steps before Leon woke up.

'Where are you going?' her husband asked in a raspy voice.

'Nowhere.'

Maree folded herself back into bed and Leon threw an arm over her. She was uncomfortable but she couldn't bring herself to say anything. This was her husband's latest, and sadly best, attempt at intimacy. Maree decided to soak it in.

***

At the breakfast table Maree and Leon found themselves alone. She looked at the difference in food before them. While he had made himself a bowl of Weet-Bix she was about to enjoy crackers with avocado and a cup of tea. Leon licked his lips as he stood up. He poured milk over his cereal before dousing it in a heaped spoon of Milo. Unsatisfied with the results he took his spoon, which still had traces of Milo on it, and dipped it into a jar of honey. Maree cringed slightly at the sugary results.

'Are you going to have time to go to the tip for me today?' she asked Leon.

'Ah maybe. I want to get some stuff done for the book.'

'It's just that some of our old stuff has been in Mum and Bill's spare room since we moved in and you told me you'd take it to the tip.'

'I will, I will! It's fine,' he said quickly, and dug into his food.

'Okay. Remember Bill can lend you his trailer.'

As if summoned by the sound of their names Bill and Val entered the room, wearing matching robes that they'd bought on a trip to Singapore, and started their breakfast routine. Maree was chewing her crackers but gave a polite half-wave of acknowledgement.

The grown-ups took their food into the living room, where they divided up the newspaper into sections. Maree knew her parents had been trying to normalise this new living situation as best they could and supply them both with a level of privacy. When they were alone again Leon piped up.

'What time do you finish work?'

'Five. Same as every day,' replied Maree, a little passive-aggressively.

'Great. See you then.'

Leon dropped his empty bowl in the sink and headed back upstairs. Val spotted Maree sitting alone and wandered back into the kitchen.

'Happy birthday love,' she said, throwing her arms around Maree from behind.

'Thanks Mum.'

'Maybe Leon's planning something for later.'

'Maybe.' She wasn't so sure.

***

Maree grabbed her travel mug of coffee from the car and stepped out. A crowd of people were gathered in the office parking lot. Maree initially thought it might be a fire drill. As she stepped deliberately around the group she was shocked to see a two-metre high portal had opened in front of their workplace.

Maree dropped her travel mug, which popped open against the concrete, spilling its contents.

'Whoa!'

Candice came over and stood next to Maree, carefully avoiding the coffee as it spread into a puddle.

'It's so wild, isn't it Maree? Have you ever seen anything like it?' she asked.

The large oval-shaped mass before them was a surreal sight.

'Where did it come from?' asked Maree as she studied the swirling green pattern in front of her.

'No one knows,' reported Candice. 'Did you see any of the others on your way in?'

'Others?'

'Oh yeah. They're everywhere!' laughed Candice, who was clearly enjoying the novelty of the moment.

One of the men in front of Maree suddenly tossed a book into the portal and they all jumped as it vanished from sight. Oddly the disappearing book made no sound.

'Are they... safe? Should we move back?' asked Maree. Instinctively she'd already started to edge away.

'I'm sure they're fine,' Candice replied in an indifferent tone.

Lachlan walked out towards them, looking impeccably dressed in a three-piece suit. He was a company man and wouldn't entertain wasting time at work.

'Maree! Candice! Let's go! It's after nine,' he called, as he waved them over.

Maree cautiously picked up her travel mug, watching the portal as she moved.

'Coming boss!' called Candice.

Maree seemed to be hypnotised. She just stood there, processing all the new information attached to this discovery.

'Can you believe him?' asked Candice, as she tossed her blonde hair up in a ponytail. 'Acting like it's just a normal workday.'

'This is so weird,' stated Maree.

'Come on,' said Lachlan, who had started to become impatient. 'Remember the *Employee of the Month* competition!'

'Maybe he hasn't seen it,' laughed Candice. 'Maybe he's going blind. He probably masturbates a lot.'

Maree tried not to laugh as they walked past Lachlan and into the office.

Candice performed a little salute to their manager as they wandered past.

***

Nobody could concentrate throughout the day. All of the sales team were glued to the rolling news coverage on their phones and computers. Marcus wandered over to Maree's desk wearing a bold red tie.

'Morning Marcus.'

'Hey. How full on are those portals?' he began. 'One appeared in my next-door neighbour's house! Like *inside* their living room.'

'My Mum just texted me and apparently there's one in my street. Candice says they are popping up everywhere,' exclaimed Maree.

'Yeah… check this out.'

Marcus showed her a video on his phone. As he held out the screen for her to see Maree exhaled nervously, their faces almost cheek to cheek. She liked being so suddenly close to Marcus. The image before her was of a French news reporter waving his arms. The next angle must have been filmed from a drone or a helicopter as it showed a stretch of land, including the Eiffel Tower, with a visible line of green portals. The portals had formed a grid, spaced evenly into the distance in all directions.

'There are reports from the US, Africa… everywhere,' said Marcus.

'So… what are they? Aliens?' asked Maree.

'I've been watching all morning and it's too early to tell.'

'Don't let Lachlan find out you've been slacking off!'

'I know,' said Marcus. 'He's on the warpath.'

'This is so strange…' said Maree.

'Some people think it's aliens, but nothing has come out of the portals yet. Some experts are saying that they are a gateway to another dimension… or a parallel world. There is rolling coverage on TV if you want to watch too,' stated Marcus.

'They just came out of nowhere.'

'Yeah and because there are so many of them the government can't stop people from getting as close as they want!' Marcus seemed excited by the chaos too. Maree reasoned that perhaps any break from the monotonous routine of sales calls was a welcome one. Candice had spotted their conversation and decided to join them.

'You guys talking about the portals?' she asked, eyebrows raised.

Maree nodded.

'I heard that the government sent drones through and lost contact with them,' said Candice.

'Yeah they did!' agreed Marcus.

'And apparently the US President wants to send through nukes.'

'Really?' Maree was amazed.

'I heard they sent through a guy in one of those old underwater diving suits with the air hose at the top,' said Marcus.

'That doesn't sound right.' Candice pulled a face.

'I'm pretty sure it is.'

'Why would they use one of those old metal diving things anyway… I mean aren't the helmets supposed to be super heavy?' asked Candice.

'That's just what I heard,' Marcus said defensively.

'Well it sounds wrong.' Candice was sticking to her guns.

Maree had been ignoring them. She'd been reading an article and decided to share it with her friends.

'It says here that they all appeared at once around 3am,' said Maree, reading off the screen. 'There's heaps of surveillance footage of them popping up.'

'I wonder what's on the other side,' pondered Candice.

The commotion of the office environment had caught the attention of Lachlan, who wandered out to address the sales team. He had a personal PA system that he sometimes used for announcements. It was always set up outside of his office. He brought the microphone to his lips, resulting in some very annoying feedback.

'Alright settle down. Let's use this worldwide event to sell some Ad time people. I know these portals are interesting and that means people are watching their TV's right now,' reasoned Lachlan, who had always had a head for sales. 'They haven't taken a commercial break yet but when the hosts get tired, and they will, the breaks will roll. Get on the phones and let's sell, sell, sell. See what you can do people!'

'What a tool,' whispered Marcus to Maree. 'I wish *he'd* piss off through a portal.' He wandered away and without thinking Maree checked out his butt. She scolded herself internally and turned back to her phone. Candice was loitering and preventing her from doing anything.

'Did you hear about Tony?' asked Candice.

'No, what about him?'

Tony usually sat at a nearby desk but there was no sign of him today.

'I overheard someone say that he got sucked into a portal last night.'

'Is that true?' asked Maree.

'Well he hasn't shown up for work yet!'

***

On the television screen a news anchor was reading from the teleprompter in front of him. He looked tired. As the rolling coverage of this worldwide event continued to unearth more and more videos and theories the anchor had been forced to report on them. Every television channel was in a standoff, each waiting for the other to blink and roll a commercial break. The veteran reporter addressed the audience at home, in the voice that had made him one of the most trusted local newsmen in the game.

'From early reports scientists have confirmed that these portals appear to have their own gravitational pull. Officials are urging people to stay inside their homes and away from the portals. I repeat, do not approach or come into contact with the portals. If you have a portal inside your home, you are being asked to stay with a relative or friend...'

***

The office fridge needed a clean. The issue was that nothing was labelled, meaning nobody knew who to blame for the excessive amount of unconsumed food. As Maree was removing her sandwich from the side of an overcrowded shelf Marcus entered the kitchen.

'Are you ready for today's question?' he asked.

'As ready as I'll ever be.'

'Now keep in mind I came up with this one before all the portals appeared, so it's not portal related,' stated Marcus.

'That's ok. It's good to have a break from all the portal-chat,' said Maree.

Marcus commented that *Portal-Chat* would make a good name for a podcast about the worldwide phenomenon. A quick Google informed them that the name had been taken, along with fifty others.

'Okay here we go,' said Marcus as he placed both hands out in front of him. 'When you plug in your phone charger at the base of the phone, from the perspective of your phone, is that more of a dildo or a butt-plug situation?'

Maree blinked hard, taken aback by the random and explicit nature of the enquiry.

'Whoa. I didn't know I would get such a philosophical question today,' she said jokingly.

'It's a good one, isn't it?' he said with a smile.

'Well I've certainly never considered my phone's point of view when I plug in my charger,' replied Maree.

'So, what do you think?'

Before she could formulate an answer, they were abruptly interrupted by Lachlan. Maree closed the fridge door and the atmosphere of the office kitchen changed.

'Thank you for that,' said Maree addressing Marcus. 'I'll take on that query and let you know if I come up with a... suitable answer for you.'

'Great, thanks Maree. I'm sure we can work it out,' replied Marcus with a smile.

'Absolutely.'

As Maree left the kitchen she heard Marcus asking Lachlan a question, and had to cover her mouth to stop from laughing.

'So how 'bout those portals?'

***

At her desk Maree received an email from Candice. These short correspondences were often trivial, and she shot her friend a look to see whether it was important. Candice watched her with wide eyes, nodding slightly as if to say *Read my email now!*

The subject line read: *Put on headphones before pressing play!* Maree sighed and complied with the request. Clicking the attached link, she hoped this wasn't a prank.

The video had been shot in New Zealand, which Maree could determine by the accents. There were a group of guys on screen wearing cargo shorts and t-shirts. The tallest of the group held a drone in his hands while another operated the remote. The cameraman filmed a wide shot of the scene as the drone flew into a portal and disappeared. They burst out laughing, throwing the drone remote in too. The group then picked up a spear gun, with a rope tied to the spear. As Maree was questioning the legality of the weapon, the group targeted the portal and fired the spear through. The rope tightened up, as if hitting a target on the other side, and then with great force the rope was sucked into the vortex, pulling the spear gun with it. All of the men in the video laughed except for the owner of the spear gun who looked upset at the loss of his weapon.

Maree's desk phone rang. It was Candice.

'Hey,' said Maree.

'Hey babe.'

They had often called each other's phones in the past as a way of covertly gossiping.

'It looked like that spear hit something, right?' asked Maree.

'Oh definitely,' agreed Candice. 'People are throwing things through portals all over the world. It's so wild.'

'But nothing is coming back out!'

'Nothing has ever come back out, no.'

'What do you think they're here for?' asked Maree.

'Only one way to find out really.'

Candice had a very devious look on her face. Maree could tell right away that she was planning something.

'No... Candice, you're not thinking of going through, are you?'

'I am actually,' announced Candice.

'Why? You don't know what they are!'

'Who cares! I don't have anything here that's worth staying for. Do you think this job is what I saw myself doing for the rest of my life?' asked Candice.

'Is this because Monica went to Paris?' asked Maree.

'This has nothing to do with her!'

'I don't think you've thought this through. I don't even want to go near those things in case they give me cancer and you want to walk *through* one? What if you get vaporised?'

'I've joined a bunch of message boards for now,' said Candice. 'I'm becoming very informed Maree. Don't worry babe I won't make any rash decisions.'

'Ok good.'

'Happy birthday by the way,' whispered Candice.

'Thank you. This is why you can't go through a portal. Nobody else knows when my birthday is,' reasoned Maree.

'I know you don't want to make a big deal of it here at work but is Leon going to take you out to dinner or something?'

'I hope so. If he remembers I guess,' said Maree with a shrug.

'Hmmm, I don't like your chances then.'

'I guess we'll see…'

Maree said goodbye and hung up her phone. When she looked back at her computer screen there was a message from Marcus.

Did I just overhear that it's your birthday???

Maree reasoned that Marcus must have amazing hearing. Either that or he'd been eavesdropping on them. She looked up and locked eyes with him. Maree nodded reluctantly. Marcus mouthed the words Happy Birthday and tilted his head to the side. Maree could feel herself starting to blush, so she gave him a smile and returned to work.

CHAPTER THREE

True to form Leon had forgotten her birthday.

'Are you serious?' he asked.

'Yeah. Today's the twelfth,' replied Maree.

Leon was sitting on the bed, computer in hand, looking confused. Maree stood in the doorway, unsure of what to do next.

'I thought it was next week,' said Leon, sounding like he was complaining.

'It's okay, really… it's fine.'

'Fuck. I feel awful,' he said. 'I was going to take you out, wasn't I? I completely forgot.'

'Don't worry about it.'

'I've been watching all these clips about the portals and I completely forgot what day it was… it's my bad.'

'It's fine.'

Leon stood up.

'No. We should go out. You're only thirty-two once.'

'I'm thirty-one,' stated Maree.

'Right…'

***

It felt so odd to Maree to be out at a restaurant with Leon. The place was empty with the exception of one other couple that looked like they might be breaking up. Just beyond the window at the side of the restaurant was a glowing green portal. Leon's face was awash with reflected light and it made him look sickly. Maree worried that she looked just as awful, but Leon didn't seem to care. Outside the portals were becoming a normal part of everyday life. Maree watched as a small group of people were throwing items like rocks into the unknown. She wondered where they might end up, and what lay on the other side.

'Where do you think they came from?' Maree asked her husband.

'I don't know. They probably live nearby and just wandered out of their houses I guess,' he replied.

'The portals. Not the people.'

'Oh.' Leon contemplated the question. 'A parallel world probably.'

Maree stared at the centre of the portal and imagined what it would be like to travel to a parallel world. She wondered whether another version of her was happily married to Leon.

'Oh, did I tell you? Our neighbours Greg and Vanessa left,' Leon said suddenly.

'They moved?'

'No, they went through the portal on our street,' he replied.

'What? Are you serious?'

Maree still couldn't believe that anyone she knew would want to jump into the unknown like that. Candice's interest in the idea had been on her mind all afternoon. It seemed so stupid, and thoughtless, to throw caution to the wind like that. Greg and Vanessa were a pleasant couple that Maree had admired from afar. The news that they would do this made her uneasy.

'They knocked on the door and said goodbye this afternoon,' reported Leon.

'Did Vanessa give back my copy of *American Beauty*?' asked Maree.

'No.'

'Goddamn it.'

'Did you lend it to her?' asked Leon.

'Yes!' said Maree, knowing that she'd definitely complained about this to Leon before. 'Ages ago. She never gave it back.'

'I'll get it back for you,' he promised. 'I'm planning on breaking the back window and moving in. I'm going to Google the amount of time you have to squat for. Then, whether they come back or not, I'll have a legal claim to their property.'

'Really?'

'Yeah! Why not? It's right next door. This might be the way we enter the property market. Apparently people are leaving vacant houses all over the place.'

'Are *more* people going through the portals? I hadn't heard of anyone going through before now,' said Maree.

'Not sure. People are definitely going missing though.'

Leon was extremely interested in the portals. Maree wished he'd pay the same level of attention to her, or to completing his novel and getting a job.

'I wish I'd have taken you here years ago,' Leon said suddenly, causing Maree to smile. It was as if he was reading her mind. Leon was showing his romantic side again.

'That's sweet,' beamed Maree, suddenly feeling closer to her husband.

'Because back then it was all you can eat,' stated Leon.

'Oh.'

'We could have had so much food!' he chuckled.

The moment had passed, causing Maree to rest her head onto her hand. Outside a teenager pushed a bike into the portal and laughed.

***

The prison warden looked uncomfortable, as though he'd never been on live TV before. Someone from the make up team had tried their best to make him camera ready, but he still stood out like a sore thumb. His hands remained awkwardly by his sides, as if he'd forgotten what to do with them. His nervous nature was understandable. The reporter had asked him to stand in front of a pack of prisoners for his interview. Each one of the inmates had the potential to create a viral moment and steal the spotlight. The prison warden spoke clearly, and remained calm but could feel sweat forming on his brow.

'...The inmates have been in a state of complete lockdown since the portal appeared in the yard. We cannot risk letting them out for any amount of time as some of them might take this opportunity to go inside this portal. Some of these offenders are serving life sentences so the idea that there is another dimension... or another world... or whatever you want to believe, is like a literal get out of jail free card. We just can't take any chances...'

The prisoners behaved for the rest of the interview, perhaps biding their time.

***

The TV in the sales office had been muted, but the team kept watching it for updates. Kevin, one of the older employees, had asked for the subtitles to be turned on, but Candice told him off, claiming that Lachlan would notice if they were all reading the screen. The boss had been on the phone for most of the morning. Now, as the afternoon of work rolled on, Candice, Maree and Marcus found themselves in a small cluster watching the communal television. Candice hadn't given Maree any indication as to her mindset. It was starting to worry Maree. Candice was never this quiet about anything.

'Are you still thinking about going in?' she asked.

'Yeah I think I will,' replied Candice.

This news, delivered so casually, was devastating for Maree.

'But what's the point? Do you have some kind of death wish?' asked Marcus, who was just hearing about this for the first time.

'It's an adventure,' Candice replied with a shrug.

'Leon said our neighbours Greg and Vanessa went through a portal,' stated Maree.

'Did he watch them go in? Did anyone video it?' asked Candice.

'No. I don't think so.'

'That's the kind of footage I need to take a look at,' announced a hopeful Candice. 'But if they didn't film it then I can still be the first.'

'I can't believe you're serious about this,' said Marcus.

'It's going to be incredible,' reasoned Candice. 'You don't even know.'

'You don't even know either!' blurted out Maree. 'It's like one of those mystery flights Candice. It's like getting on a plane and not knowing the destination at all.'

'And the plane is a glowing portal that might kill you instantly,' added Marcus.

'People die instantly all the time. I might get hit by a bus tomorrow,' said Candice.

'But this is throwing yourself *under* the bus,' said Maree.

'It's suicide,' added Marcus. It now felt as if they were ganging up on Candice.

'You can stay here in your safe little lives then. No one is forcing you to go,' said Candice, who was getting visibly annoyed.

'But we'll never see you again! Doesn't that bother you?' asked Maree.

'Of course. But you can't ask someone to stick around just because it makes your life easier. Not if staying makes them unhappy,' said Candice.

'So you're decided? That's that?'

'Yep. And I definitely want you to film me going in.'

'How morbid,' said Marcus.

'For the last time I'm not going to die!' shrieked Candice. 'And I want you to upload it online, so everyone remembers me. I'll be famous, even if I'm not around to see it.'

Maree shook her head a little.

'I still feel like you're doing this because of Monica. I have some annual leave saved up. I'll go to Paris with you-'

'No! This is my destiny,' interrupted Candice.

'You know I saw some footage of an upcoming fashion show that's taking place in a warehouse that has a portal in it. The models have to walk around a runway that goes right around a portal,' said Marcus.

'Why are you telling me this?' Candice asked.

'I dunno. You do modelling, right? I thought maybe if you were one of the models in the show that you could just jump in while they are televising it. Then Maree doesn't have to film you.'

'They would never have me in any fashion show in my current condition!' said Candice, before storming off and leaving Marcus and Maree alone.

'Geez. What's her problem?' he asked.

'She thinks she's fat,' said Maree.

'She's obviously not fat.'

'I know. She can't be convinced.'

'Who's Monica?' asked Marcus.

'The bane of her existence.'

'Fair enough. So, Tony didn't come in again today?'

'No. Maybe the rumours are true,' said Maree. Tony's desk was empty, without explanation. Marcus scanned the room for their manager. Lachlan was still on the phone in his office.

'Hey, you want to do today's question?' asked Marcus.

'Sure.'

'Would you ever go through the portals?'

'Absolutely not,' stated Maree.

'Really? I thought with Candice going that might change your mind.'

'No chance,' said Maree. 'The idea seems crazy to me. What about you?'

'Nah… I have a life here, you know? Friends and family would miss me too damn much. I'm kind of amazing,' he said jokingly.

'Sure, of course,' she said with a chuckle.

'There is still a lot I want to do while I'm here, you know?'

Marcus paused and stared at Maree. She hoped he was feeling the way she had started to feel, and that the unspoken subtext of his words was clear to them both.

'Yeah. I know what you mean,' she said.

'Hey how was your birthday?' he asked, changing the subject just before it could become awkward.

'Just another day really.'

'You didn't do anything special?'

'My husband and I went to dinner,' said Maree.

'That's pretty special.'

'It didn't feel like it.'

Marcus furrowed his brow.

'Can I be honest Maree?'

'Of course.'

'Sometimes I don't think you're as happy as you could be.'

'Ha. Yeah that's probably true.'

'So, don't you want to change things?' he asked.

Maree considered the question.

'Sometimes I do. I want Leon to be more like he used to be when he was working. He used to have a bit more structure to his day. I'd be happy if he just made more of an effort, you know? I don't want to nag him all the time. Sometimes I think I'd settle for him doing the dishes or picking up after himself!'

'Well that's just it: You shouldn't have to settle,' said Marcus.

'For better or worse, right?'

Suddenly Lachlan materialised from thin air and interrupted their conversation.

'Sales, Sales, Sales, Sales,' said Lachlan, emphasising each word with a clap of his hands. 'That is how you win Employee of the Month.'

'Yes boss!' said Marcus, saluting for effect.

Maree smiled politely and picked up her phone.

CHAPTER FOUR

You might be afraid of what you cannot know,

The number of portals continues to grow,

But if you can't find what you need in this place,

Then jump inside a new time and space.

Jump - we'll be immortal,

Jump - and we'll be free,

Jump into my portal,

There you'll find me.

There you'll find me.

***

Maree thought the old woman across the street must have been at least eighty years old. They'd never met but she'd often watched her, watering her garden at night. She had long grey hair, down to her waist, and wore her woollen robe like a uniform. Maree had been staring out at the portal initially but kept watching when the old lady appeared. She wondered whether she had a husband, or whether she was a widow. Perhaps she'd never been married at all. Maree stared as the figure sprayed water across the flowerbeds one by one. Then the old woman noticed the portal, maybe for the first time. She approached it, squinting as she did. Maree held her breath, as if something amazing were about to happen. The woman sprayed her hose at the portal, which seemed to have no effect. Then the two locked eyes. Maree froze in the window, unable to stop staring at her neighbour. The old woman squinted back at her. Just then Val touched Maree's shoulder, startling her back to reality.

'Sorry love,' her mother said apologetically.

'It's okay. I'm okay.'

'Are you joining us for dinner then?' asked Val.

'That would be great Mum. It's been a long day,' replied Maree as she got her bearings.

'And Leon?'

'He's asleep. He was up all night watching videos of portals.'

'Isn't he supposed to be up all night writing?'

'I can't really blame him,' said Maree. 'We are living in a moment of history right now. My grandchildren will ask me about this. Where were you when the portals appeared?'

'You have to have children before you can have grandchildren,' said Val as she raised one eyebrow.

'Mum…'

'Val? Is Leon joining us?' Bill called out from the other room.

'Not tonight,' shouted Val. 'Just three plates please!'

'And Leon's trying to sleep, so maybe we could stop shouting?' added Maree.

'Sorry love.'

'It's okay,' said Maree, suddenly feeling bad for scolding her mother in her own home.

'Do you want to have children with Leon?' asked Val. She placed one hand on her hip as she waited for an answer.

'I think so. It's just a weird time with him being out of work and us living here and with the portals and everything,' replied Maree. She felt like she was trying to convince herself. It had been a long time since she and Leon had discussed having a family. It had been a long time for a lot of things. Val gave a brief nod and led Maree to the dinner table. Bill was serving himself some potatoes when they arrived.

'Those portals,' started Val as she sat down, 'they're a right nuisance, aren't they? The Smith's have one in their backyard apparently. Right above their pool! They can't use it anymore.'

'They're evenly spaced all over the world. Nobody can explain them,' stated Maree.

'Well we can't know everything about everything. Just leave them alone and they will go away on their own, I think,' said Val.

'Thanks Bill. It looks delicious,' said Maree with a smile.

'See Val?' said Bill. 'You didn't think I'd use the cookbook Maree got me, but I did!'

'You can cook every night then, aye?' said Val.

'Only if Maree joins us!' he replied.

'Let me taste it first then I'll let you know,' said Maree.

'I knocked before but Leon didn't answer. Is he out?' asked Bill.

'He's sleeping,' said Val, who sounded a little condescending.

'That's lazy,' added Bill.

'He was up late,' Maree said defensively.

'How can you spend any time together if you're living in two different time zones like this?' asked Bill.

'We are still figuring things out,' replied Maree.

'You probably should have figured things out before you got married,' stated Bill.

'Come on now,' scolded Val.

'It's like having a ghost in our attic. We never see him, we just hear him pacing around from time to time,' said Bill.

'Leon's been going through… a tough time,' said Maree, half speaking about herself.

'He needs a job,' said Bill.

'Leon's working on his novel,' Maree said quickly, even though she completely agreed that her husband should be seeking employment. She needed to speak for Leon, as he wasn't there to defend himself against the attacks.

'He can do that on the weekend. He should be supporting you. Or is that not the role of a husband these days?' asked Bill, before consuming a spoonful of peas.

Maree felt defeated. She looked down at her food and didn't say anything. Her mother could sense Maree's inner turmoil.

'It's been an adjustment having you move in with us, I'm sure,' started Val. 'We've loved having you here but it would be nice to see you both a bit more often. Together, you know?'

'I'll see if Leon can come down for dinner tomorrow night,' offered Maree.

Bill exhaled; suddenly realising he had caused some unnecessary tension.

'I didn't mean to be rude,' he said, looking upset with himself.

'It's okay. I get it.'

'I'm not feeling particularly hungry. Excuse me,' said Bill. He covered his plate with a tea towel and left the room. Val and Maree sat too quietly, as the next noise they heard was a toilet seat dropping down and a fan turning on.

'Straight to the toilet,' said Val with a shake of her head. 'He'll be in there for a half hour I reckon. Longer if he's got his phone!'

'Gross. I'm trying to eat here,' replied Maree, who now had an unappealing visual in her mind.

'Don't worry about Bill. I think he's still mad he didn't get to walk you down the aisle. Even though he's not your *real* Dad he would have loved that, you know. Since he hasn't got any kids of his own.'

When Leon and Maree had decided to get married they didn't want any fuss, as they couldn't afford to throw a big celebration. Maree had liked the idea of eloping initially because she didn't want to be the centre of attention. Perhaps in retrospect she'd worried that someone would have tried to talk her out of it. Val and Bill had been disappointed when they'd heard about the wedding after the fact. Maree found herself apologising for it regularly.

'It was really sudden,' said Maree.

'I know I remember,' replied Val with a nod.

'Otherwise, of course I would have invited you both.'

'Well, maybe we can come to your next one.'

'Mum!' cried Maree. 'That's a horrible thing to say.'

'Are you happy honey? Because we don't see how you are when you're alone. If you tell me you're happy I'll leave it be.' Val looked concerned.

'We will be,' stated a determined Maree. 'I think Leon just needs to finish this book. When he took the redundancy money I guess he thought it would last longer than it did. And when we lost our place I think he felt a bit like he'd failed.'

'Is that what he said?' asked Val.

'Well, no. We haven't really talked about it.'

'It's never easy when you lose your job,' said Val.

'Obviously neither of us thought we would be starting our married life living here, not that we're not grateful. I think Leon has just regressed a little,' offered Maree.

'That's why he needs to start up a new job. I agree with Bill,' said Val.

'I have to let him finish his book first.'

'Well how long is that going to take?'

'I honestly don't know,' replied Maree.

Val shook her head.

'I'll tell you what; if we get through that cookbook before Leon finishes his novel, you'll know he's not taking it seriously,' said Val.

'He's taking it seriously. I promise.'

'What's it about anyway?'

'It's a science fiction thing. He's been really secretive about it,' said Maree.

'Is it about the portals?' asked her mother.

'That would be some amazing foresight... but no. At least, I don't think it is. He's been writing it for a few months now. Before the portals appeared.'

'Well I hope he lets you read it soon.'

'Me too.'

'Well just remember... when it comes to a marriage it's a marathon not a sprint. Things can get better with time,' said Val.

'They didn't get better with you and Dad.'

'Your father and I were beyond saving. It takes two to make a marriage and he wasn't in it for the long run. Sometimes you have to cut your losses,' said Val, a faraway look in her eyes.

'Would you have done it differently? If you'd known then what you know now?' asked Maree.

'Of course not. Then I wouldn't have you. Or Bill!'

'Bill's great and I'm really glad you're happy but do you think you tried... you know... *everything* to make it work with Dad?'

'That was so long ago now,' stated Val.

'I know.'

'Your father and I fell out of love with each other and neither of us wanted to admit it for a long time.'

'I guess I've just been thinking about him lately,' said Maree.

'Well don't. He's not worth thinking about.'

Maree could hear Leon's nose whistling. She didn't want to wake him, but it was extremely hard to ignore. She rolled onto her side and looked at her phone. A message from Marcus.

Did you hear about Candice?

Maree was suddenly filled with concern. She glanced back at Leon before replying.

WHAT? No???

She patiently waited as the familiar typing dots danced across her screen. She felt a little scandalous texting Marcus from her bed, with her husband sleeping beside her.

It's nothing bad. Well, it is. She's set up a Facebook event.

Maree navigated herself to Facebook and found the event. Candice was advertising a farewell party for herself. The details stated that she would be leaving *this realm* and jumping through a portal. The event seemed to have a lot of interest from the media, and had been shared many times. She texted Marcus again.

We have to talk her out of it.

He replied almost immediately, as though he was expecting that response.

We won't be able to. She's made it public now.

It was frustrating. Maree was sure that the portals were dangerous, and that Candice was throwing her life away. She texted frantically.

She doesn't know what she's doing!

She's a grown woman. We can't stop her. Marcus replied.

Maree texted a sad face emoji.

Don't worry. You'll still have me to keep you company at work. typed Marcus. Maree was considering how she should respond when Leon rolled over and sniffed the air like a puppy. She quickly turned off her phone and hid it. Maree's nervousness at being discovered informed why she felt so guilty about talking to Marcus. She liked him more than she should.

***

Lachlan's office had a motivational poster on the wall. Maree couldn't help but stare at it as her manager reviewed a document.

Courage is knowing what not to fear – Plato.

She couldn't decide whether it was at all applicable to a television sales office. There was very little bravery involved in selling advertising space to prospective clients. Her eyes wandered back to Lachlan, who looked like he needed to pluck his eyebrows.

'As always, the purpose of these performance reviews is so I can be alerted to any issues that are affecting my staff and deal with them,' he said, addressing her in his most managerial tone. 'Is there any pressing issue that you need me to address in this workplace?'

'Nothing comes to mind.'

'Nothing since the last review?' he asked.

'The last review was only a few months ago,' she replied.

'So, the frequency of reviews bothers you?'

'I didn't say that.'

'Look Maree I respect your work ethic. You're one of the good ones.'

'Thank you.'

'That being said you've never made enough sales to win Employee of the Month. I'm happy to tell you that this month is particularly close, and you have a good chance of winning.'

'Ok great.' Maree forced a smile.

'It's just that I worry that you're becoming distracted. Candice in particular seems to be a distraction for you. Would you agree?' asked Lachlan, his unplucked eyebrows now raised.

'No. I don't feel distracted by her.'

'She wears inappropriate attire...'

'She wears business clothes,' said Maree, jumping to Candice's defence.

'Yes but they are all... tight... and distracting,' he replied.

'I disagree.'

Lachlan shuffled a few papers into a neat pile.

'Look I probably shouldn't be telling you this yet but there will be a new supervisor position advertised in the coming weeks and I think you'd be very well suited to it,' he said.

'Oh... thank you.' This was a genuine surprise for Maree. A promotion would mean more money, which could lead her to move out again with Leon. She had no idea that Lachlan viewed her as supervisor material.

'But it would be much easier for me to recommend you to the higher ups if you won the Employee of the Month award,' added Lachlan.

'I see.'

'So maybe you could spend some more time pushing ad sales instead of watching those portal videos.'

'I don't-'

'I see what goes on in this office you know,' said Lachlan, interrupting her. 'I see the emails and the video links.'

'I'll try and make some more sales Lachlan,' she said submissively.

'It would be in your best interests.'

'Thanks for thinking of me.'

'Like I said, you're one of the good ones. I have to take care of the company's future,' said Lachlan.

He signalled that the performance review was over, and she stood up to leave.

'I don't think you'll have to worry about Candice distracting me for much longer anyway,' she said as she headed for the door.

'Why is that?' Lachlan looked perplexed.

'She's not going to stick around.'

'Is she resigning?'

'Worse… she's decided to jump into a portal,' stated Maree.

'That the most ridiculous thing I've ever heard.'

'I know. That's what I've been telling her.' Maree thought quickly and edited herself. 'When we talk about non-work-related issues at lunchtime or after work that is…'

Lachlan looked stunned.

'When is she planning on doing this?' he asked.

'Tomorrow night. She's having a farewell party.'

'I hadn't heard.'

Lachlan rubbed his temples. He looked concerned, which made Maree uncomfortable enough to leave the office.

***

Candice had headphones on and was staring at a news report when Maree walked past. She could see the graphic on the screen:

Scientists have no new information.

Candice spotted Maree and pulled off the headphones.

'How was the performance review?' asked Candice.

'Fine,' replied Maree. 'Apparently I might win Employee of the Month.'

'And then all your dreams will have come true!' her friend said sarcastically.

'Lachlan was right; you're very distracting,' stated Maree.

'Oh, you love it.'

'Have you changed your mind yet?' Maree had been trying to talk some sense into Candice all day.

'Nope. I'm definitely going.'

'Are you sure? You'll miss out on your quarterly performance review,' said Maree, in a jokey manner.

'I think I'll miss those least of all,' said Candice with a laugh.

Maree thought she felt her phone vibrate in her pocket. She checked it and found it was only her imagination.

'Expecting a call from the hubby?' asked Candice.

'Sort of. We haven't spoken much recently.'

'He's been up writing?'

'Actually, I think he's been up watching portal videos,' said Maree.

'What's his book called again?'

'Don't ask me that,' said Maree, screwing up her face, 'I don't know anything about it.'

'But it's sci-fi?'

'That's right.'

'Do you think it will be any good? I mean, has he ever written anything before?' asked Candice.

'Nothing that I've read,' said Maree.

'No love letters then?' teased Candice.

'Not lately.'

'He's too busy watching portal coverage?'

'He is very interested in them,' stated Maree.

'Who isn't?' laughed Candice. 'Have you let him see *your* portal lately?' Candice followed her enquiry with a derogatory gesture towards her lap.

'Don't be gross.'

'I'm just saying maybe you should jump him. Give him something to write about.'

'I'm going to ask him if I can read some of it. The curiosity is getting to me,' said Maree.

'Good. Hey… so speaking of portals… there still aren't any videos of people going into a portal voluntarily. I've been looking for them online every day,' said Candice.

'There is probably a good reason for that!'

'I'm going to be like Neil Armstrong.' Candice was beaming. There would be no changing her mind now. Maree knew she had to keep trying anyway.

'Except you won't come back,' said Maree.

'But everyone will know my name!'

'Not worth it.' Maree shook her head.

'If you ever get sick of it here, you're welcome to jump in after me,' said Candice.

'Well it's nice to have options. Hey… why are you still coming to work? If you're jumping through the portal isn't this more pointless than usual?' asked Maree.

'I don't have the Internet at home. That's the main reason I usually came in here anyway, and to see you of course! Alright, I'll catch you later.'

'See you Candice.'

After her friend left the office Maree returned to her desk to find a card tucked underneath her mouse pad. She instinctively knew it was from Marcus. She tucked it into her bag and tried not to blush.

CHAPTER SIX

On the television screen a policeman was addressing a room full of reporters. The occasional flash from a photographer gave the scene an old timey feel. He stood at a podium, fielding questions from various media representatives. In front of him, attached to the podium, were nine microphones. Each was branded with a different news or radio channel's logo.

'No, I can neither confirm nor deny that,' the policeman said. 'Next question please?'

'How are you planning on keeping citizens safe?' called out one of the reporters.

'At this time we are policing the streets around the portals, with additional patrols in metropolitan areas, but as you know nothing has come through them. We have been asked to stress that the police will not be attempting to enter any portal as our jurisdiction is strictly in this dimension... here on Earth. We will be working with the community to secure the portals and make them as safe as possible. We ask for your cooperation as we prioritise the worst affected areas.'

***

Maree walked into the bedroom carrying a plate of food for Leon, who was seated in his usual beanbag chair on the floor. He put down the book he was perusing, and she passed him a plate. Without a comfortable second seat Maree decided to sit cross-legged on the floor.

'Thanks for getting this for me babe,' said Leon.

'You know we really have to eat downstairs one night this week.'

'Sounds good.'

'Promise?' Maree needed her husband to be a more active member of the household.

'Yeah absolutely.'

'Oh, but we can't tomorrow night because we're going to Candice's farewell,' said Maree.

'Oh right. Do I have to come to that?' asked Leon.

'Yes. I'd like you to.'

'I mean... I don't really know Candice,' he protested.

'But I want you to be there.'

'I'll guess I'll try.'

'Why can't you take the night off from writing?' asked Maree.

'I'm just really in it right now, you know? I love what I've written so far, and I think it's really good.'

'That's good. I'd love to read some.'

'No worries,' he replied nonchalantly.

'No, really,' she said, stressing the words. 'I want you to let me read some. I don't even know what it's about.'

'Okay, sure.'

'I mean, what's it called?' she asked.

'I haven't given it a title yet,' replied Leon.

'Okay, but what is it about?'

'The human mind and its infinite capabilities,' he stated.

'Okay...'

'I'll let you read some soon.'

'Is there a main character?' asked Maree.

'I'm the main character.'

'So… it's biographical?'

'No, it's science fiction. I haven't mastered the infinite capabilities of my mind.' Leon rolled his eyes.

'And the main character is named Leon?'

'Yes.'

Maree felt like she was no closer to finding out anything about his secret project.

'This sounds confusing,' she said.

'It's pretty complicated.'

As she watched her husband stuff food into his mouth she wondered about his story. If it was biographical, that only raised more questions.

'Am I in the book?' asked Maree.

'A little… at the start,' he replied with a mouth full of food.

'Well that's the part I want to read.'

'Soon, okay?'

'Okay. I'm going to go take a shower.'

***

A News reporter stood outside a bar surrounded by a rowdy crowd. She struggled to report her story, doing her best to ignore the escalating scenes behind her.

'It is believed that tonight Candice Monroe will jump into a portal voluntarily,' she said, ignoring the sound of breaking glass somewhere in the distance. 'We will attempt to talk to the young woman before she jumps but we have been told that she is not suffering from any medical conditions and she is choosing to do this in sound body and mind.'

***

Maree spent much too long getting ready, but now that she'd probably be interviewed by the media, she had decided it was worth it. The bar was almost at capacity although somehow everyone from work seemed to have made it past the bouncers that were located at every exit. The atmosphere surrounding the bar was one of excitement and intrigue. Candice told Maree that she'd selected this establishment due to its proximity to one of the portals, which could be seen through the windows of the establishment. It bathed most of the crowd outside in an eerie green glow. All around her Maree could see dancing and yelling. At the centre of the room was her best friend Candice. She loved the attention and hugged people one by one. Candice was dressed all in white, as though she was marrying herself. Maree scanned the room but did not see Leon. She decided to text him:

What time are you coming???

A finger tapped Maree on the shoulder. She turned to find Marcus holding out a drink for her. He looked equally overdressed.

'Thought you might like a drink,' he said with a smile.

'Thanks Marcus.'

'Is your husband coming?' he asked.

'I really don't know anymore.' Maree exhaled. 'I thought he was, but he hasn't been answering my texts today.'

'I'm sure he'll turn up.'

'Maybe.'

From out of nowhere Candice shimmied up and threw her arms around them both. Candice was powerfully drunk. Their three heads were now pressed close together due to the excessive force she was using on them.

'It's really happening you guys! It's so wild!' said Candice.

'So wild,' repeated Marcus.

'How are you feeling?' asked Maree.

'Oh my God, so so good!'

'This is a great party Candice. Did you get some kind of sponsorship to pay for all this?' asked Marcus.

'Nope!'

'So...'

'I maxed out my credit cards!' said Candice with a laugh.

'Seriously?' asked Maree. Candice was making messes that she wouldn't be around to clean up. Maree thought she was being too reckless and inconsiderate. She gave Candice a disapproving look.

'I know! I spent fifteen thousand dollars!'

'Well this is going to be one hell of a party,' stated Marcus.

'Probably for the best that you're not going to be around when the bill comes then,' said Maree.

'I'm going to miss you two sooooo much,' said Candice.

'I'll going to miss you too Candice,' replied Maree.

Candice had released them now and she turned her attention to Marcus.

'Promise me you'll take care of Maree for me, okay?' she said, spitting a little.

'I will,' he replied.

'Promise me!' pleaded Candice. 'Make sure Lachlan doesn't give her a hard time.'

'He doesn't give me a hard time,' chimed in Maree.

'He's a jerk!' screeched Candice.

'I heard he's here somewhere,' said Marcus.

'Is he?' Candice searched the room. 'I didn't invite him.'

'Well, he probably heard about the party anyway,' argued Marcus.

'How did he get past security?' Candice asked nobody in particular.

Maree shrugged.

'Lachlan?' yelled Candice.

'Wow,' said Maree, holding her ear. Candice had shouted right into it but was oblivious in her intoxication.

'I'll chat to you soon babe,' said Candice as she stumbled away.

'So how have you been?' asked Marcus.

'Fine. I mean… I haven't been sleeping as much as I'd like,' she confessed.

'Why not?'

'I don't know! Could be stress I suppose?'

'You have a lot on your mind now that you're thirty-one huh?'

'It's like I start thinking about everything right as I'm trying to sleep. And that makes me anxious,' said Maree.

'I feel like my mind has been racing lately, you know?' said Marcus.

'Yeah?'

'Yeah. Just buzzing. I have all these ideas,' he said.

'That's cool… I guess.'

'I had my performance review with Lachlan, and he told me, confidentially of course, that I'm in line for a promotion to supervisor.'

'Did he?' asked Maree with wide eyes.

'Yeah isn't that great?'

'*So* great.'

There was no reply from Leon. Maree decided to give up and just enjoy the party. This was Candice's moment. Her own marital issues could wait. The crowd had mellowed and thinned out. While the turnout had been overwhelming at first, the security guards had kept the onlookers outside and they had become restless. The crowd that waited now consisted of only about fifty people, not including the reporters. The DJ had changed the music to create a more relaxing vibe, and Candice had sobered up. Maree hoped she might change her mind and stay.

'Well it's almost midnight!' announced Candice.

'And Cinderella has to go?' asked Maree, sensing the answer.

'Well I only have the venue til midnight,' she said.

'And I'm guessing the media won't wait all night,' added Maree.

'Hey… thanks for making that sales job so bearable for all these years,' said Candice, giving her a hug.

'It has been bearable, hasn't it?'

'Just.'

'It's not too late to back out you know,' offered Maree.

'I know you can't understand this… but I just have to do it. I'll always regret it if I don't,' stated Candice.

The two hugged again.

'You're a beautiful friend Candice. I hope you find what you're looking for on the other side of that portal.'

'Oh, I think I will Maree. And if I'm wrong at least this was fun while it lasted. Speaking of fun… are you having any?'

'I'm having a nice time,' replied Maree.

'Marcus has been following you around like a lost puppy,' said Candice with a grin.

'At least I've had someone to talk to. Sorry… it's just that Leon should have been here to say goodbye.'

'Who cares about that guy? You need to stop apologising for your husband.'

'It hasn't been easy for him.'

'Stop it. You're doing it again!' said Candice. 'He didn't want to be here, and I don't care that he's not. I just care about you.'

'I know.'

'Look, I hope he finishes his book or whatever he's doing and snaps out of it. If he doesn't though you need to start worrying about yourself, okay? There are plenty of fish in the sea,' said Candice.

Out of the corner of her eye she saw Marcus. Maree knew that he was the fish Candice was referring to. She started to feel guilty again.

'I love you Candice.'

'I love you Maree. Oh, and I got you a little going away present too.'

'What is it?'

'I also used my credit card to buy up a bunch of ad time for you. So you would win Employee of the Month,' stated Candice.

'What? You did not!'

'I did. The paperwork is at your desk at work. It's in Leon's name and I said it was to advertise his upcoming book release.'

'Oh wow…' laughed Maree.

'So he'd better finish it because the advertising is all paid for,' said Candice with a smile.

'Thanks. You're the best.'

'You're welcome. Now it's time to say goodbye.'

Candice stood up on the nearest table and clinked her glass with a fork. The remaining crowd cheered, alerting the cameramen and the reporters outside that the jump time was nearing.

'Thank you all so much for coming tonight,' said Candice. 'It makes me feel really special that so many of you decided to come out to see me off. I love you all!'

'Love you Candy!' called a man in the crowd.

Suddenly Candice's eyes went wide and she pointed towards the back of the room.

'YOU!' she said, climbing down from the table. Candice strolled ahead and the crowd parted to reveal Lachlan, standing alone by the bar. The room looked confused.

'Hello Candice. Nice party,' he said.

'Thanks. I don't remember inviting you,' she shot back.

'I know. I just heard you were leaving… and I needed to see if it was true,' said Lachlan.

'And you just snuck in?'

'No, I gave the security guard a generous tip and he let me in.'

'Huh. That's a pretty boss move.' Candice put her hand on her hip and smiled.

'Thanks.'

'I like that you don't care what people say about you.'

'What do people say about me?' asked Lachlan, looking confused.

Candice didn't answer. Instead she stepped towards him and kissed him deeply. The crowd had a mixed response of cheering and jeering. Maree was surprised at the level of affection between them. Lachlan kissed Candice back for a while before breaking the kiss. He looked like he'd been holding his breath and only just realised it.

'That was nice,' said Candice.

'Yes, it was,' panted Lachlan.

She kissed him once more and then walked outside to address her public. The reporters immediately started asking questions, but Candice ignored them until she had positioned herself in front of the portal. Maree and Marcus followed her out. Candice had bought an expensive High Definition camera for the event and given very specific instructions to her friend about how to film the scene. Maree gave her friend a thumbs up when she was rolling. Candice had pre-recorded a farewell package for Maree to upload with her footage, ensuring hers would be the official version, despite the reporter's additional angles.

'Ladies and Gentlemen… the time has come,' said Candice, playing up dramatically for the camera.

'Candice are you scared?' asked one of the reporters.

'I'm not afraid of anything!' she said.

'What do you hope is on the other side of the portal?' asked another reporter.

'A world full of equality and happiness for all!'

The reporters all started talking over one another, each vying for the next question. Candice put her hands on her hips and held her pose. Maree thought she looked empowered, like a superhero.

'I love you all!' said Candice.

She offered the crowd a peace sign and threw herself dramatically backwards into the portal.

CHAPTER EIGHT

The crowd gasped and then cheered. The reporters started filming their sign offs and concluding materials. Maree kept filming the scenes, hoping that if one day Candice was able to return, she could show her what happened next. One of the drunk patrons threw a beer bottle into the portal. With the spectacle now over the crowd started to dissipate. Soon the only people outside besides the press were Maree, Marcus and Lachlan.

'I can't believe she did that,' said Lachlan. He looked forlorn.

'Neither can I,' said Maree.

'She kissed me.' With that statement Lachlan wandered away into the night in a daze.

'See you on Monday Lachlan!' called out Marcus.

Maree and Marcus stood in front of the portal as the news reporters packed into their vans and drove away.

'Quite a speech. I guess Candice was big on... *equality?*' asked Marcus.

'I guess equality is important,' said Maree.

'Did you get it all on film?'

'Yeah. I'll post it tonight.'

The two watched the swirling green mass. It was hypnotic, like a lava lamp.

'I'm sure she's in a better place,' said Marcus.

Maree screwed up her face at his poor choice of words.

'Really?' she said.

'I don't mean a better place like that. I don't mean that she's *dead*. I'm sure she's alive,' he said, backpedalling.

'You can't be sure.'

'Okay, I'll just jump in and check!' he said and jokingly took a step towards the portal. Maree reached out and grabbed his hand, pulling him back towards her. Marcus interlocked their fingers and kept holding her hand. There was electricity between them.

'I don't know what I'm supposed to do anymore,' confessed Maree.

'Nobody does.'

'I'm just tired, you know?'

'It's been a big night,' agreed Marcus.

They stood for a moment longer as Maree enjoyed holding his hand. It then occurred to her that they were standing far too close to the portal for her liking.

'Should we move away from the portal?' she asked.

'Yeah...'

They stopped holding hands and took two deliberate steps back, continuing to admire the unexplainable vortex.

'It's beautiful, isn't it?' asked Marcus.

'If you like green.'

'Oh, I do.'

'Then it's very beautiful,' said Maree with a smile.

'Candice is so brave,' he said.

'She was.'

'She *IS*,' said Marcus.

'Maybe she'll be the first person to come back through a portal,' said Maree.

'If anyone can do it it'll be Candice.'

'Yeah.' Maree didn't believe her words but tried to remain hopeful.

'Do you know what I think these portals are?' he asked.

'No, what do you think they are?'

'Possibility.'

'Possibility?' she asked, confused.

'Since the portals appeared I kind of feel like anything is possible,' stated Marcus. He put one arm around Maree and hugged her.

'That's terrible,' she said.

Marcus let her go.

'What?'

'Possibility? *Really*?'

'I thought it was thought provoking!' he said.

'It was cheesy.'

'Maybe a little.'

***

Maree was exhausted. Each step up the staircase to her bedroom was more effort than the last. When she crept into the room she was surprised to see Leon, fully dressed, looking upset.

He was sitting on the bed with the light on, as if he'd been waiting for her return.

'Where were you?' asked Maree.

'I didn't feel like going to a party,' replied Leon.

'Why didn't you text me back? I was looking for you all night.'

'Don't lie to me.'

Maree was taken aback by this statement.

'I'm not lying,' she said. 'I kept calling you.'

'Until you stopped…'

Maree didn't like his tone.

'Well… answer your phone then!' she replied.

'What's the point?' he seethed.

'What's wrong with you?'

'I found this yesterday,' said Leon, holding up the birthday card from Maree's bag.

'So?'

'So, who's Marcus?' he asked.

'A guy from work,' replied Maree. While she'd always relayed stories about Candice or Lachlan, Maree had never spoken to her husband about Marcus. She'd been afraid of her two world's colliding, and the way her husband would react.

'Is he the guy who was all over you tonight?'

'What are you talking about?' Maree swallowed nervously.

'I saw you with him. I saw the two of you holding hands. You *like* him, don't you?' asked Leon.

'You were there?' Maree felt angry. She wondered how long her husband had been spying on her.

'Don't change the subject!' shouted Leon.

'He's just a friend,' said Maree.

'I don't believe you.'

'Nothing has happened between me and Marcus.'

'Not yet, but It's only a matter of time, isn't it?' Leon's eyes were wild.

'Well, at least he remembered my birthday… and came to the party. I can't count on you for anything lately.'

'Just say it. You don't want to be with me anymore,' stated Leon.

'You're my husband. Of course I do.'

'But do you still love me?'

'You're making it so difficult,' replied Maree.

'What is that supposed to mean?'

'The man I married was full of ambition. Where's he gone?'

'I'm writing a book!' stated Leon defensively.

'Are you? Let me read it then!'

'It's not ready.'

'Yeah? Well it sounds like a stupid idea to me,' she said.

They were trying to hurt each other now. Maree felt so exhausted. The fact that she couldn't go straight to sleep was making her even angrier.

'You're just not smart enough to understand it!' said Leon sharply.

'That's a really nice thing to say to the woman you're supposed to love!' replied Maree.

'You're the one attacking me.'

'I've been asking you to clear out the spare room for weeks,' said Maree, airing out more grievances.

'It's done. I did it today,' he replied.

This took her by surprise. Maree walked out of their bedroom and checked the spare room. It was empty. He had cleared it out. She returned to Leon.

'Did Bill end up lending you his trailer?' she asked.

'I didn't need it.'

'Then how did you get it to the tip?'

'I didn't take it to the tip,' replied Leon.

'What?'

'I threw it in the portal.'

'You dumped our old furniture into the portal?' asked Maree.

'It was garbage.'

'And I asked you to take it to the tip.'

'I got rid of it… just like you asked!'

'That's not what I asked for!' screamed Maree.

'Well, it's done now, isn't it?'

'You half-ass everything, do you know that? You're half-assing this whole marriage!' Maree could feel her blood boiling.

'You'd know about that. You've been looking for a way out since I got made redundant,' said Leon.

'No, I haven't! I've been supporting you. You've been in a hole since we moved back here. I've been trying to pull you out of it!'

'You wanted me to clear the spare room and it's done. Why aren't you happier about it?' asked Leon.

'Because you're lazy,' replied Maree. 'And I'm sorry but you do the bare minimum. You were talking about squatting in Vanessa and Greg's place? Have you broken in and started squatting yet? Did you find my copy of *American Beauty*? Have you even Googled how long you would have to squat in their place for?'

'No… I haven't broken into our neighbours place yet.'

'And you won't because you don't do anything,' said Maree.

'This is why I've been avoiding talking to you,' he said suddenly. 'I knew we'd fight.'

'Well you haven't really given me an alternative, have you? But I'd rather stay up fighting than not talk to you Leon.'

'This isn't how I thought married life would be,' he said.

'Then why were you in such a rush to marry me?'

'Because I loved you…'

'I think you were being selfish,' stated Maree.

'What do you mean?'

'You just didn't want anyone else to have me.'

'That's not true. We were happy.'

'But getting married isn't the finish line. You can't just stop trying,' she said.

'If you didn't want to be with me then you shouldn't have said yes.'

'Sometimes I wish I didn't.'

Just then Bill opened the door without knocking. He looked very tired.

'Maree, it's four in the morning. We're trying to sleep,' he said in a croaky voice.

'Sorry Bill,' said Maree.

'Yeah, so sorry Bill. It won't happen again,' called Leon as he pushed past both of them and headed downstairs. Maree followed him outside. Leon started to pace in the front yard, looking distraught with his hands over his head.

'Come back inside,' said Maree.

'Forget it,' he replied.

'Don't be stupid. I want to work this out.'

'Everything I do is for you!' said Leon. 'Do you know how much it hurts me when you say I don't have any ambition?'

'I might know how you felt if you ever talked to me! Let me in!' she begged. Bill and Val were now watching from the upstairs window. The fight had also attracted the attention of the old woman across the street, who was staring at them from her doorway.

'You're making a scene. Please come back inside,' she pleaded.

'Do you still love me?' asked Leon.

Maree hesitated and then answered.

'Yes.'

'Tell me the truth,' said Leon.

'I am.'

'I don't believe you.'

Leon started running away from her. In an instant Maree realised where he was headed.

The portal.

'Leon wait!' she called.

It was no use. Leon was determined to leave, ignoring her cries. Maree felt helpless as her husband leapt into the air and disappeared into the portal.

'Noooooooooooooo!' screamed Maree, as she collapsed onto the lawn. She wanted to stand up and chase him into the unknown, but she was too afraid. Her body wouldn't allow her to move.

CHAPTER NINE

The sales manager Lachlan stood at his personal PA device and spoke to his team. They were all gathered around, facing his office door and awaiting some potentially good news.

'Thank you all for your hard work this month. There has been renewed interest in television advertising thanks to the increase in rolling coverage and some of you were able to capitalise,' he said. It was true. The entire world had been glued to their screens in anticipation. From out of nowhere glowing green portals had invaded the entire planet. Nobody could explain them, and some people had become so curious that they dove into the unknown in search of answers.

'This brings me to the Employee of the Month,' continued Lachlan. 'This person has shown a high level of professionalism. This person is one of the best in the sales team. Please join me in congratulating Maree on her first Employee of the Month award!'

There was a light smattering of applause as Maree stumbled over towards Lachlan. She looked like she'd been awake all night, with dishevelled brown hair and a shirt in desperate need of an iron. Maree snatched the award from her manager's hand and shuffled away without uttering a word of thanks.

***

Maree watched as two birds hopped dangerously close to the nearby portal. If one of the birds accidently went in, she wondered whether the other would instinctively follow. She hadn't followed her husband Leon when he'd jumped and for the past week she couldn't stop asking herself why. Maree was sitting underneath a tree, covered in crumbs from her lunch, when Marcus wandered towards her. She knew she didn't look good, but she didn't care anymore. Leon was gone. He'd left her alone, preferring to throw himself into a portal than stay and be married to her. She took a quick swig from her water bottle as Marcus approached. The bottle was full of rum.

'Hey Maree. Congrats on winning Employee of the Month,' said Marcus cautiously.

'Thanks. It's all Candice's fault. She bought a bunch of sales for me before she left so that I'd win,' replied Maree. She missed Candice a lot, but she wasn't mad at her for leaving. At least she'd had the courtesy to say a proper goodbye. The birds that Maree had been watching suddenly flew away.

'Are you doing okay?' asked Marcus.

'You don't really have to check up on me. I know Candice told you to look after me but I'm fine,' said Maree.

'I'm not checking up on you because of that. I care about you.'

For Maree it felt like the end of the world. She was running out of people to talk to so Maree decided to confide in Marcus.

'Leon left me.'

'Oh my God, that sucks.'

'I got home after Candice's party and we had a fight.'

'Do you want to talk about it?' asked Marcus.

'Yes, *obviously*!' she shrieked. 'I'm talking about it now!'

'Sorry, sorry. Go on. You had a fight?' asked Marcus.

'A big one. He walked out the front door and threw himself into the portal on our street.'

'Whoa.'

'Can you believe that?' asked Maree, brushing some of the crumbs off her arm.

'No. I mean… I didn't *know* him but I'm shocked,' replied Marcus.

'It's over,' stated Maree dramatically. 'He's probably dating someone new over there in some other dimension and I'm stuck here.'

'I'm sorry. That really… sucks,' repeated Marcus. 'But maybe this is going to turn into the best thing that could have happened.'

'I don't know about that.'

'Well I do.'

'He's such an arsehole.'

'I know he is. He's a stupendous arsehole. Hey… maybe you should take a couple of days off?'

'No! If I do that then he wins!' cried Maree. She shook her metal water bottle to confirm to herself how much rum she'd consumed so far. It was about half full. She picked up the remaining sandwich and took an incredibly small bite. Marcus noticed her odd manner of consuming food and commented on it.

'Why are you taking such tiny bites of that sandwich?'

'It makes it last longer,' said Maree.

'You know no one is really monitoring the length of your break. You can take as long as you like out here.'

'If I eat slowly I enjoy it more.'

'But can you even taste it?' asked Marcus. 'You're barely eating any of it.'

'I've survived this long, haven't I?'

'Okay, eating habits aside, seeing as how you've clearly had a few drinks maybe you should just take the rest of the day off. I can drive you home,' he offered. 'I'll tell Lachlan you're not feeling well.'

'I don't care what he thinks…'

'I know… but let's get you back home anyway,' said Marcus.

'Okay, but you have to drive my car for me so I can get to work tomorrow,' she said, slurring her words.

'Alright I'll do that but let's just worry about one day at a time. Come on, let's go.'

Marcus helped her up and together they walked towards her parked car.

***

Maree stared out of the window, lost in her own world. It felt strange to see Melbourne whizzing by from her passenger seat. This change in perspective made things seem *off*. Maree couldn't stop thinking about Leon and everything that they'd lost when he'd abandoned her.

'If we had a baby I was going to name her Emily,' she blurted out.

'What's that?' asked Marcus.

'If Leon and I had got pregnant and I'd had a girl I was going to name her Emily.'

'And if it was a boy?'

'I don't know. I guess it doesn't matter now,' Maree said with a sigh.

'You can still have a baby. You're only thirty.'

'I'm thirty-one…'

'So, there's plenty of time,' said Marcus.

'I don't want to have a baby by myself.'

Marcus went quiet. She wanted him to say something profound to make the pain of abandonment go away. Maree wanted him to hold her and make her forget about Leon. While she craved more from Marcus, she also worried that it was too soon to move on. The car drove past another glowing portal.

'It's so weird how everyone has just accepted that there are portals everywhere,' said Marcus as he observed how commonplace the green ovals now seemed.

'There's not much we can do about them is there?'

'I suppose not.'

'So, if there's nothing you can do then you just have to accept it,' said Maree.

'And move on?'

'Maybe.'

'Do you want to know what my favourite quote is?' asked Marcus.

'I guess.'

'It's from Winston Churchill I believe. He said: "If you're going through hell, keep going." I love that quote. Maybe you're almost coming out the other side, you know?'

'I get it…' offered Maree.

'Don't you like it?'

'It's stupid. Next you'll tell me that every cloud has a silver lining.'

The car rolled forward steadily and Maree took a large swig from her bottle.

'I'm so sorry that this happened to you,' Marcus said sympathetically.

'Yeah? Well I hope he's dead.'

'No, you don't.'

'I do!'

'If Leon is dead then Candice is dead.'

Maree knew he was right. She didn't want her best friend to be dead, so she altered her argument.

'Fine… they're both alive, but Leon is hurt.'

'Yeah, maybe he landed on a rock,' offered Marcus.

Maree smiled a little at the visual.

'This is my place up here. Turn left.'

Maree stumbled out of the car and immediately tripped into a flowerbed near the letterbox. She started swearing and Marcus rushed to her aid.

'Here let me help,' he said.

'I'm fine,' said Maree. She'd trampled a cluster of daisies. Her head was spinning, and she felt like she might be sick at any moment.

'I know you *think* that…'

Marcus helped her to the front door and pressed the doorbell. He was surprised when a very burly man, shaped like a potato with thick black hair protruding from his nostrils answered the door.

'Yes?' he said, scratching at his hairy left forearm.

'Hi. Just bringing Maree back home,' said Marcus.

'Who?' The man stared at them blankly.

***

'Now you're sure *this* is your house?' asked Marcus who was rapidly learning that one of the dangers of driving a drunk person home was their terrible sense of direction.

'That's the one,' replied Maree.

'Number four?'

'Yes.'

'You're sure now?'

'YES! *Geez*,' replied Maree aggressively.

It was the third house they'd tried and thankfully on this occasion Maree's mother Val opened the door for them.

'Maree?'

'Hi there. I'm Marcus. Just bringing your daughter home,' he said.

'Hi Mum,' slurred Maree.

'Have you been drinking?' asked Val.

Maree nodded.

'She's a bit under the weather, yes,' replied Marcus.

'Thank you. I'll take it from here,' said Val, shooting both arms out towards them.

He transferred Maree's floppy body over to her mother and then took the car keys from his pocket.

'I'll just give the keys to you,' said Marcus.

Val suddenly realised that he'd driven Maree's car.

'Oh, thanks for driving her home. I don't drive anymore but I could ask my husband to drop you somewhere,' offered Val. She turned her head back inside the house and shouted for her husband.

'BILL!'

Marcus smiled politely.

'BILL?' she called again.

There was no response. Maree shifted nervously. She was certain that Bill was otherwise engaged in the toilet, which made her feel even more embarrassed.

'Can I get him to drop you off somewhere? asked Val, turning her attention back to Marcus.

'Thanks, but I'll be fine. See you at work Maree,' he replied.

'Thanks Marcus.'

***

The spare room had been transformed since Leon emptied it out. In front of Maree now sat a large table, with a five-thousand-piece puzzle spread across it. Val returned with two cups of sleepy time tea.

'Marcus seems like a nice boy,' she said, clearly fishing for more information.

'He's very nice,' replied Maree in a robotic tone.

'It was good of him to drop you home.'

'Uhuh.'

'And he has those gorgeous blue eyes. Those are nice, aren't they?'

'I hadn't noticed,' lied Maree.

'Are you going to make a habit of this? Drinking during the day?' asked Val.

'I don't think my body could sustain it,' said Maree as she propped her head against her hand. She could feel a headache approaching.

'Good. It doesn't suit you,' stated Val.

Maree let out a heavy sigh.

'Are you sleeping any better?' her mother asked.

'No.'

'Can I be honest with you?'

'Yeah...'

'I never really liked Leon for you,' said Val.

'Don't say that Mum.'

'Why not?'

'Because it will be really awkward when he comes back,' answered Maree.

'I think we both know he's not coming back. Even if he crawled back through a portal now, he's not welcome in this house. Not after the way he's treated you.'

Maree picked up the top of the puzzle box and stared at the skyline of Seattle. The Space Needle was prominently in the foreground of the scene.

'How is this any fun?' she asked, changing the subject. Maree had never understood the appeal of doing a puzzle. Her mother regularly brought home old ones from the op shop. She'd finish them and then return them like a library book. Maree always thought the second hand puzzle would be missing a piece but they never were.

'I enjoy it. If you enjoy something then it's fun,' replied Val.

'But you can see what it's going to be on the box.'

'It's more about the journey love. Sometimes you still want to finish the puzzle... even just so you can see the whole picture. There is a sense of accomplishment in that.'

'It doesn't sound very satisfying,' said Maree.

'Well maybe you should find your own hobby then... and stop trashing mine,' Val replied defensively.

CHAPTER TEN

That night Maree couldn't find any sleep. One drink became five and before she knew it, she was standing outside in her pyjamas. She stared at the portal that had consumed her husband. The portal that ruined her marriage. It looked exactly the same as it always had but she now viewed it as smug. She attributed that this alien portal was now pleased that Maree was alone. It swirled happily, waiting for its next victim. Maree took a swig from the wine bottle that she'd carried outside before tossing it into the centre of the green mass. It disappeared without a sound, leaving Maree unsatisfied and alone in the street.

***

The male reporter couldn't believe his luck. He was standing next to an attractive model in an exclusive backstage area, behind the catwalk that she had just ventured down. He smiled as he asked her questions, wishing privately that every day at work could be as exciting as this one. The model wore a t-shirt that said *TEAM CANDICE* on it in sparkling letters.

'And did you speak to Candice in the hours before she jumped?' the reporter asked.

'I did. Candice and I were *soooo* close. She was my best friend,' the model replied.

On the screen a graphic revealed her name to be Monica Sanders.

'And how would you describe her temperament in the lead up to her now infamous jump?'

'She said to me "Monica, I want you to tell my story," and I was totally into it.'

Monica pouted for the camera.

'And, that's why you've written this book?'

'That's right,' she replied.

Monica held up a thin book called *Friendship across Dimensions*. On the front cover was a photoshopped image of Monica posing with Candice.

***

Maree sat at her desk playing with a pencil. She wobbled it up and down as she waited for the day to be over. She loathed work now that Candice had escaped the daily grind. Maree spent a lot of her day wondering where her friend had landed. She felt sure that Candice was alive, but without jumping in after her she'd never know for sure. There had been a lot of copycats in the wake of her video going viral. When Maree casually searched the Internet now there were hundreds of videos of people going through portals. Candice would have loved it, wherever she was.

Maree glanced across the room and was surprised to spot Tony sitting at his desk. There had been speculation that he'd gone to the other side - which is what people had dubbed the journey through the portals - but there he was, sipping from a glass bottle of pineapple juice.

'Tony?'

'Hi Maree. How have you been?' he asked, as casually as ever.

'We thought you were dead!' exclaimed Maree.

'Um… I've been on annual leave.'

'So, you weren't sucked into a portal?'

'No. Lachlan knew where I was. If you needed to know you should have just asked him.'

'Well, welcome back,' said Maree.

Tony started drinking the pineapple juice again and caught Maree staring at him.

'It's my birthday on Thursday,' he explained, before taking another swig.

***

Candice's farewell video had accumulated millions of views. Maree must have been responsible for at least twenty of those. She lay in her bed alone, trying to distract herself from Leon's absence. She clicked the play button and watched Candice on the screen.

'I'm not afraid of anything!' her friend said.

Maree paused the video and replayed the statement.

'I'm not afraid of anything!'

Maree smiled. Her friend posed like a superhero, gave the peace sign and jumped to the other side. She scrolled down through the sea of comments below the video. There were thoughts and opinions from people all over the world.

What a babe.

Such a waste.

RIP Candice.

Peace!!!

Too bad those portals are only ONE WAY!

What an idiot. I hope she's dead.

Maree shut her computer and rolled over. The bed was spacious without Leon. She still wasn't used to being alone in it. Maree wondered if she'd ever get used to it. Now that she was finally free to do anything, she didn't know where to start. Leon's pillow still smelled though, so Maree closed her eyes and pretended he was still next to her, snoring peacefully.

***

In the shared office kitchen Maree waited while her lunch heated up in the microwave. She was feeling tired again and had started to wonder if there was a support group for people dealing with loss. She was still angry with Leon but with each passing day it was lessened. Marcus wandered into the room and interrupted her daydreaming.

'How are you feeling?' he asked.

'Fine. That wasn't today's question of the day was it?'

'Nah. Did you want today's question?'

'I don't know Marcus. Your questions are usually so stupid,' she blurted out.

'Whoa. Tell me what you really think!' he said with a laugh.

'Sorry that was mean. I'm just tired. Go ahead... what's your question?' asked Maree.

'Would you let me take you out to dinner sometime?'

'What?'

'Will you go to dinner with me?' asked Marcus.

'Um... like a date?'

'Yes, like a date. Let's just have dinner and we'll see how it goes.'

'I don't know. Let me think about it.'

'Okay.'

'You're really sweet to ask but I'm not sure...' she let her voice trail off.

'I understand. Think about it.'

'I will.'

Maree wondered whether she should jump into something new. She liked Marcus a lot, and her husband wasn't coming back. Without Candice at work they'd become closer. This worried Maree, as if things went south they'd still have to see each other every day. She ate her lunch at her desk and fantasised about starting a relationship with Marcus.

CHAPTER ELEVEN

Maree shattered the glass and waited. She had expected to hear a curious neighbour approaching to investigate the sound, but nobody came. She reached her hand in through the broken window and unlocked the door. No alarm had been set at Vanessa and Greg's house. They must not have cared what happened to their residence. The place was completely abandoned, which made her sad. She'd always liked them as neighbours. When Maree and Leon had first moved back into her parent's place she'd fantasised that the four of them would go on double dates together as couple friends. In reality Vanessa and Greg had liked to be alone. Maree couldn't think of a time she'd seen them apart. They liked each other so much in fact that they'd jumped through to the other side together.

Hanging in the living room, as if to mock her unsuccessful marriage, was a large photograph of the happy couple. Vanessa was playing with one of her blonde curls while Greg stood happily beside her. Maree felt tears forming in her eyes but she shook them away. She remembered the purpose of this break-in and scanned the shelf in front of her. Maree tossed item after item onto the cream coloured carpet. If they didn't care about any of this stuff then neither would she. Maree stopped when she found her DVD copy of *American Beauty*. She had loaned it to them ages ago and Vanessa had claimed that it had been returned. Maree laughed to herself.

'I knew it.'

She ransacked their kitchen, taking several bags of chips, and walked back to her parent's place to watch the film.

***

On the screen Carolyn Burnham, portrayed by Annette Benning was addressing her husband Lester, who was played by Kevin Spacey.

'Don't mess with me Mister, or I'll divorce you so fast it'll make your head spin!' spewed Carolyn.

'On what grounds? I'm not a drunk, I don't fuck other women, I don't mistreat you, I've never hit you. I don't even try to touch you since you've made it so abundantly clear just how unnecessary you consider me to be!' replied Lester. 'But I did support you when you got your licence, and some people might think that entitles me to half of what's yours. So, turn out the light when you come to bed!'

Maree took another swig of her alcoholic drink. This movie used to be a guilty pleasure of hers but now it only served to remind her of the fragile nature of relationships.

***

On the screen a group of guys in backwards hats were taking turns doing trick shots. They would take a basketball or a football and hurl it through an impossible number of obstacles towards a portal. Each time it went in successfully the group would cheer and high five each other. The video promised to be the first in a series of trick shot portal videos.

'And that's how it's done!' yelled one of the guys at the conclusion of the vision.

Portals were more popular than ever. There were hastily manufactured versions of portal themed paraphernalia popping up everywhere.

How to bake a portal cake, portal inspired makeup, speculation videos about the other side, bumper stickers, T-shirts, podcasts, music videos, conspiracy theories and so much more.

Maree was constantly distracted by the portals and felt like she couldn't escape their influence. The green grid stretched everywhere that she went, and they made her think about Leon and Candice. She wondered if the two of them had found each other on the other side. Leon had never been good at recognising her friends, so she doubted he would have remembered her. Maree considered that Candice probably would have found the coolest crowd over there and made an impact. Maybe they were on an alien planet and Candice, being one of the first arrivals, was now famous.

Maree still searched online for new and interesting videos about the portals in her downtime. She knew that she was really searching for proof that something, or someone, could come back. She wanted to know if her husband would come back to her. It was feeling very unlikely.

***

Val and Maree were sitting in the kitchen and admiring the food that Bill had made.

'I hope you're hungry,' said Bill, setting down dessert. He'd baked an apple pie from scratch and the smell was divine.

'We sure are!' Val replied for them both.

Her parents had both been surprisingly nice to Maree and she'd felt much better thanks to their hospitality. They hadn't hidden their delight that Leon had departed but seemed to silently agree that the best thing to do was to keep on going. It was just like the Winston Churchill quote that Marcus had mentioned. *If you're going through hell, keep going.* It had grown on her and she now felt like she was coming out into the light again. Maree had decided not to follow her husband into the portal, which meant that her life would continue here without him. This revelation had been dawning on Maree slowly, but she'd accepted it now. It wasn't the end of the world, just the end of their marriage.

The newspaper had been left open in front of Maree. On the page was a political-style cartoon of a man in a reclining chair watching TV. Appearing to be fed up with what was before him the caption said: *Ugh, Portals again?*

The man in the recliner was tossing his remote control over his head into a nearby portal that was located directly behind him in his living room. Maree smiled at the sentiment. These portals were everywhere, and everyone was sick of talking about them.

Val tasted the first course and made a loud and satisfied sound.

'Delicious! You're getting better at this every day,' she exclaimed.

'You're not just saying that now?' asked Bill.

'Mmmm, it's really good,' agreed Maree, after trying the dish.

'My husband the chef!' Val smiled proudly.

Maree watched as her parents embraced. They still looked at each other as though it was only their third date. Maree folded her arms and admired the scene in front of her.

'You two are lucky. You make marriage look easy,' she proclaimed.

'Well it helps when you're with the right person,' stated Val, before giving her husband another kiss.

'That's nice.' Bill looked chuffed.

'I didn't think I'd ever get married again after your father. Bill had to talk me into it. It's taken us years to get to where we are now. It doesn't just happen without work you know,' said Val.

'And it nearly didn't happen at all,' remarked Bill.

'What are you talking about?' asked Maree.

'Haven't I ever told you this story?' Bill looked bemused.

'You know, I don't think we have,' mused Val.

'What story?' Maree had no idea what they were talking about.

'Your mother and I met on a blind date. I'll never forget it as long as I live,' said Bill.

'Neither will I!' said Val.

'So, your mother walks into this bar wearing this gorgeous dress. She looked amazing.' Bill smiled at the memory. 'And she comes up to me and I am speechless.'

'I apologised for being late, which I was... quite late... and I start rabbiting on about something or another...' said Val, continuing the story,

'And she shakes my hand and we order a drink,' said Bill, seamlessly picking up the tale. 'And it's not until the end of the night that she asks me if I'd ever been on a blind date before. I didn't realise that this was supposed to be a blind date!'

'My real blind date was sitting somewhere in that bar and he must have thought I'd stood him up,' commented Val.

'He certainly missed out!' said Bill.

'It was the best mistake I ever made.' Val smiled to herself. Maree nodded in agreement. Their happiness couldn't be denied.

'We never looked back after that. You say I had to convince you to marry me?' said Bill.

'You did. I wasn't sure!' confessed Val.

'Well I was. Nothing had ever felt so right before,' Bill replied.

'I guess some things just happen when you least expect them,' said Val, as she cleared the table.

CHAPTER TWELVE

Maree was lying in her bed with her eyes open. Her insomnia felt like it was all consuming. Suddenly the bedroom was bathed in green light, which startled her. A green portal had opened horizontally, just above her bed. It appeared to be floating, flush with the ceiling. Maree stared into it, before hearing a voice.

'Maree…'

It was faint but it sounded like Candice, calling to her from far away. She wanted to fly up and into the unknown, but Maree felt fused to her bed. A gust of wind seemed to throw papers and clothes around the room in her peripheral vision. Maree couldn't break eye contact with the portal. It spun hypnotically and expanded in size before her. Soon her entire ceiling was spinning. Maree woke up in a cold sweat. The room was impossibly still, as always.

***

Maree was eavesdropping on her co-workers instead of doing her job. She was quietly seething and now that Candice had departed she couldn't vent her frustrations. She found everyone around her to be irritating except for Marcus. No more than five feet from her desk a small group of her colleagues had gathered around Tim, who was telling them an incredibly loud story. Maree had started grinding her teeth subconsciously.

'So my bank card is about to expire, and like a good customer I pop into the bank and wait in line and I say to the teller my card is about to expire and I just want to check you have the right address on file,' says Tim, addressing the group. 'She confirms my address, and it's right. So, I go on my way. The day my card expires arrives and I still haven't got a new card. So, I go back into the bank and wait patiently and I'm like hey, I still haven't received my card.'

'Unbelievable,' Jane from Accounting chimed in. Kevin nodded in agreement while sipping his coffee.

'I know!' exclaimed Tim before continuing. 'She apologises and says it should arrive in the next day or so. Well it's Friday and I need money for the weekend, so I get some cash out. My card doesn't come on Monday, Tuesday or Wednesday and I'm fuming. They tell me to be patient and that it's in the mail. I walk across the street to another bank and I open an account. They give me a card straight away.'

Maree looked up at the faces of her co-workers to find them enthralled. She screwed up her face, wondering how this interaction could be considered anything but dull.

'I go home and start transferring money five hundred dollars at a time to my new bank account. Five hundred dollars a day every day until the old account is empty. When the money is all gone, I go back to my bank and I say 'Hey, I still haven't received that card.' They play dumb and tell me it must still be on the way. I say forget it. I've moved on. I've got a new bank now and I'm here to close my account with you! God it was so satisfying. But you know what the worst part was? When I was closing my account they went to confirm my address and it was the wrong one. They sent my card to the wrong address! That's what I went in to check in the first place!'

Maree couldn't take it anymore. She stood up and vented her frustrations, using every curse word she knew.

***

It felt like Maree and Lachlan were in a staring contest that she was losing. The only sound in the manager's office was the ticking of a clock on the wall. Lachlan's features were remarkably still and Maree wished he hadn't elected to pucker his lips quite so much. She waited patiently to hear how much trouble she was in.

'This is unacceptable behaviour,' said Lachlan, unfolding his arms.

'I know.'

'I would have expected this kind of outburst and foul language from Candice but not from you.' The way that Lachlan said Candice revealed venom behind the word. He was upset with her.

'Sorry.'

'You used to be an exemplary employee. What's changed?' asked Lachlan. 'Is this because Candice left?'

'I...'

'Big deal!' said Lachlan as he interrupted her. 'You can't get attached to people. Sometimes they leave.'

'It won't happen again,' stated Maree.

'Of course not... people can't leave twice...'

'I meant the... *outburst*.'

'Right,' said Lachlan, as he pursed his lips again. 'See that it doesn't. Tim won't be filing a complaint. That's the silver lining.'

Suddenly the whole situation seemed ridiculous to Maree. The world was so different now. Portals had opened up, revealing the probable existence of alien races or at the very least alien technology. Her best friend was in a parallel world, or another dimension or goodness knows where. And here Maree sat, being reprimanded about her language, and Tim wasn't even going to make a formal complaint about her. Her outburst didn't even matter to him. She'd been saving for her future with Leon. Now that her husband was no longer around she felt silly. She wondered what she was doing with her life. Maree burst out laughing, causing her whole demeanour to change.

'What's so funny?' demanded Lachlan.

'You. You're acting like nothing's changed. There are portals all over the world and you think I'm worried about Tim filing a complaint? Who cares! None of this even matters,' said Maree with another laugh.

'It does matter.'

'It doesn't!' she said defiantly.

'Careful Maree. You'd better change your attitude or you're going to find yourself unemployed.'

'Thanks boss. Great pep talk,' said Maree, before marching out of the office. She spotted Marcus heading towards the men's room and followed him. Maree was feeling reckless, so she decided not to let a little thing like bathroom etiquette stop her. She crashed through the men's room door, startling Marcus. Without saying a word Maree threw her arms around his neck and kissed him deeply. He took her by the waist and kissed her back. Maree was surprised by how amazing and right it felt.

'Still want to take me to dinner?' she asked when the kiss ended.

'Yes.'

'It's a date,' she confirmed.

'Great.'

'Great...'

They stood facing each other for a moment, perhaps unsure of what to say next.

'This is awkward. I came in here 'cause I have to use the toilet,' said Marcus, screwing up his face.

'Oh, right… sorry.'

Maree hadn't experienced any nervousness about the date until the doorbell rang. The sound seemed to vibrate throughout the house and into her bones, both exciting and startling her. She opened the door and was pleasantly surprised to see that Marcus had made an effort. She appreciated his salmon blazer, and felt less overdressed in her black dress because of it.

'Hi Maree,' he said in a tone that she found seductive.

'Good… *great* to see you,' she managed to say, despite her nerves.

'You look great.'

'Thanks, you look good too,' she said, feeling herself blush.

'Shall we go?'

With that her mother appeared and intruded on their conversation.

'Oh hi! Marcus, isn't it? How are you?' Val asked casually.

'I'm well, thanks,' he replied.

'I'm Val by the way. We didn't really get a chance to meet properly when you dropped Maree off the other day. Thanks again for doing that.'

'It was my pleasure really.'

'Okay… we should be going,' Maree said quickly, feeling embarrassed at both her mother's intrusion as well as being reminded of her recent day drinking.

'Are you going out anywhere special?' asked Val.

'Just an Italian restaurant,' replied Marcus.

'Oooh… that should be nice. Don't fill up on bread, will you?' advised Val with a smile. Maree rolled her eyes.

'Okay Marcus let's go.' She walked away from her mother briskly.

'Have a good night,' Marcus said to Val, before following his date.

'Stay out as long as you like,' called Val.

***

The Italian restaurant had six other patrons. Maree wondered whether the portals kept people indoors or whether they'd stayed away from this establishment specifically. The atmosphere that was being created with dreadful elevator music didn't make Maree hungry. Bracketed to the wall was a television, displaying footage of the deserts of Egypt from a helicopter. On the screen a line of now familiar green portals stretched off into the distance. Despite her mother's warnings Maree was eating bread from a basket in small but satisfying bites.

'So, what do you think you'd like to order?' Marcus asked, as he flashed her a smile. Maree thought he looked gorgeous. She smiled back without showing her teeth. Maree was determined to see whether this flirtation between them was worthy of further exploration.

'I don't know. Back when we went to restaurants… when we first started dating… Leon and I used to order two different things and eat off each other's plates,' she replied.

'That's one way to do it, sure.'

Maree mentally kicked herself for committing such a cardinal first date sin: *Thou shalt not discuss your ex.*

'But we didn't go to restaurants very often,' she said quickly, trying to clarify and recover from her faux pas.

Marcus nodded and looked at the menu.

'Do you know what you want?' she asked.

'I do!' replied Marcus. 'Every time I go out for Italian I have the carbonara.'

'*Every* time?'

'Yes, every time.'

'Don't you get sick of it?'

'No. I guess I'm the kind of guy that finds one thing he likes and sticks with it,' he said.

'How admirable,' said Maree as she pulled the strap of her dress back onto her shoulder. 'Well I'd get bored of carbonara. Pasta is too heavy to have all the time.'

'Well I jog every morning. And I only take special ladies to Italian restaurants, so I don't eat it that often.'

'Naturally! Wait, you jog *every* morning?'

'Yeah I'm up at five.'

'Ugh, I'm not a morning person at all,' said Maree, although after she'd said it, she wondered if it was still true. The insomnia she'd been suffering from had really wreaked havoc on her body clock.

'Sunrise is a beautiful time of day,' said Marcus.

'So is sunset,' she countered.

'Touché.'

Marcus and Maree took a sip of wine at the same time maintaining eye contact as they did. She became self-conscious and blinked first.

'I've been thinking about our kiss,' said Marcus.

'Me too.'

'You have?'

'Yeah. I've never kissed anyone in the bathroom before,' said Maree. 'I'm kind of regretting that.'

'Oh really? Don't regret it. I loved it,' said Marcus.

'There was probably faecal matter in the air.'

'Ugh. No...' Marcus screwed up his face.

'Anyway, sorry,' said Maree, shaking her head. 'I should just shut up.'

'No, it's fine,' said Marcus. 'The last date I went on brought up faecal matter too so, it's fine.'

'Oh God,' said Maree, putting her head in her hands. She was not used to dating, and she wished she was better at it.

'You're very cute, you know that?' said Marcus.

'Don't say that...'

'I mean it. You're easy on the eyes Maree.'

'Thanks.'

She was pleased that Marcus seemed to be having a good time, despite her bringing up such unpleasant visuals.

'Ahem.' Marcus cleared his throat expectantly. Maree was confused.

'What?' she asked.

'This is the part where you compliment me.'

'Oh... I see what's going on here.'

'You do?'

'Yeah... this wasn't about complimenting me as much as getting me to compliment you!' chuckled Maree.

'In your own time,' prompted Marcus playfully. He was enjoying himself.

'This still feels sort of strange,' confessed Maree.

'Was that your compliment?'

'No!'

Marcus took another sip of wine. Maree had initially feared that he would spill some on his salmon jacket, but he proved more than capable of drinking like an adult. Everything Marcus did felt refined and mature when compared to Leon. He seemed to have answers and was actually listening to her when she spoke.

'How is this strange?' he asked, staring at her with his intoxicating eyes.

'I still feel married, you know?' Maree had started fondling her wedding ring. She'd been unable to take it off.

'Leon has been nothing but selfish. It's not the way it should have ended between you two,' said Marcus.

Maree nodded in agreement. Leon's actions did seem selfish in retrospect. He'd left her in the middle of a heated argument, during a moment of sleep deprivation and hurt. Maree had often wondered whether he'd regretted his decision to go, and hated that they couldn't speak about it.

'Sometimes I wake up and for a few minutes I forget that he left, you know?'

'Sure. That must be hard,' said Marcus.

'It is.'

The waiter walked by without engaging them. Maree was glad, as she still didn't know what she wanted.

'It's over though, isn't it?' said Maree with a sigh.

'Yeah. I'm sorry.'

'This *sucks*.'

'I'm here for you Maree. I'm not going anywhere, okay?'

'I know. It feels like you've always been there, haven't you? In the background...' Maree had realised that Leon wasn't coming back, and that perhaps her future was sitting right in front of her.

'I'm still waiting...' he said.

'I know.'

'For my compliment...' said Marcus.

'Ha.'

Maree took a sip of wine as she studied the face before her. He was handsome and she wanted to tell him so, but she didn't want to give away how much she liked him. Marcus held her gaze patiently, enjoying having an excuse to stare.

'You have nice blue eyes,' she said finally.

'I hear that a lot,' he replied with a pleased smile on his face.

***

Marcus parked his car in front of Maree's place beneath an overcast sky. She looked out of the car window at the moon. It was barely visible through the clouds. She wondered whether the Earth looked different from space now. She imagined that a grid of portals would create a glowing green effect, but she hadn't seen any images like that in the media. Maree looked up at the night sky and hoped that somewhere up there an astronaut had the answer. She turned back to Marcus and smiled.

'Thanks for tonight. It was surreal going on a date again,' she said.

'Well I'd like to take you on another one… if you'd let me.'

'I think I'd like that.'

'Good.'

'Do you think we're rushing into this?' she asked.

Marcus shook his head.

'No. I like you… you like me. Why waste time?'

Maree fiddled with the wedding ring on her finger. She was so much more aware of it now, after drawing attention to it at the restaurant.

'If you want to take things slow that's fine too,' he offered.

Maree slid the ring off her finger and placed it in her handbag. She bit her lip and then leaned in and kissed Marcus on the mouth.

'Or faster is fine too,' he said after their kiss was over.

Out of the corner of her eye she thought she saw a flicker of movement from the window. Were her parents checking in on her?

'I can't invite you in. My Mum would love that a little too much,' said Maree.

'I do tick a lot of boxes, don't I?' joked Marcus.

'Don't get cocky.'

'Okay.'

They kissed again, which made Maree conscious of how lonely she'd been since Leon had left. She'd longed to be touched. This connection was welcomed, and it made her feel human again.

'You're a good kisser,' she said with a smile.

'Thanks.'

He was kissing her with such gentle and restrained passion that she wanted more. Maree hadn't felt wanted like that for a long time. Too long, she decided.

'I have another idea,' she said, opening the car door. 'Come with me.'

***

Nobody had fixed the broken glass panel at Vanessa and Greg's place, which was not surprising. Maree carefully guided her hand through, opened the door and stepped inside.

'Watch out for the glass,' she advised Marcus.

Maree tried a light switch, but the electricity had been disconnected. She stepped on something rough in the dark, which caused her to awkwardly bump into Marcus. She held him in the dark, and they embraced each other again. Everything that she'd thrown to the floor when she had searched for the *American Beauty* DVD was still there. Each knick-knack now presented an obstacle for the two of them to avoid as they shimmied their way towards the sofa.

Once they'd arrived on the leather seats Marcus immediately increased his interest in Maree. The strap on her black dress had slipped, which led him to tenderly kiss her neck and shoulders. Maree ran her hands along his back as he pulled her closer. Marcus shifted her body in one swift movement and suddenly they were horizontal. His intentions were now clear, and a delighted Maree moaned softly. They were discovering each other like teenagers, as they fumbled in the dark.

Suddenly there was a noise from the other room. It caused them both to look up like a pair of meerkats.

'Does someone live here?' whispered Marcus.

'It's abandoned,' said Maree. 'They went to the other side.'

A shadowy silhouette flickered past them, moving quickly through the living area and out the front door. The room was instantly flooded with moonlight, revealing amateur graffiti on the walls. Someone had been in there, looting and vandalising the place before Marcus and Maree had interrupted his adolescent crimes. While she was in a state of shock at the encounter, Marcus yelled out and followed the culprit outside. Maree watched from the doorway as a teenager ran away with a black plastic bag. He sped past the portal in the middle of the street and disappeared around a corner.

'Are you okay?' asked Marcus, returning his attention to her.

'Yeah I'm fine. What did he steal?'

'I didn't see. He had it in a bag,' he replied with a shrug.

The moment was lost, and Maree decided to be sensible.

'I think we'd better call it a night,' she said, staring past Marcus at the portal.

CHAPTER FOURTEEN

Maree had been lying on the floor and throwing a ball into the air like some kind of prisoner. She misjudged one throw and the rubber ball bounced off her shoulder, landing underneath her bed. When Maree turned her head to the right in search of the ball, she saw Leon's laptop computer. The white light nodded on and off in front of Maree, drawing her attention. She dragged it out, placed it on top of the bed and opened it. There was no password and Leon's screen did not feature any image as its wallpaper. The battery was running low, so she plugged the computer into the wall and started her search of its contents. Maree could see a folder titled *Writing*. She opened it and saw a Microsoft Word document called *Novel*. Maree hesitated for only a moment before opening the file. Leon's unfinished manuscript filled the screen before her and she gleefully devoured it, her eyes darting from left to right in rapid succession.

***

Lachlan had been promoted into management four years earlier. There was a rumour that he'd called a meeting every Friday since that promotion, and that felt accurate to Maree. Her boss was a creature of habit and he seemed to thrive on order. He'd once again decided that the best way to communicate with the staff as a group would be to use his personal PA device, while the employees seemed to have mastered the art of ignoring him until the meeting was over.

'So, if you could all sign the card for Tony… I'll leave it here near the water cooler. I understand he'll be off work for at least two weeks,' said Lachlan.

Maree hadn't been paying attention and didn't know what had happened to Tony. She folded her arms and glanced over at

Marcus who was wearing a full suit. This was unusual and she wondered whether he had a job interview or a funeral later on. Maree thought he looked good.

'And finally, the Supervisor position has been filled internally and I'm happy to inform you all that Marcus will be second in command as of today,' stated Lachlan.

She realised his new attire had been intentional. This was Marcus trying to look managerial. The rest of the sales team groaned audibly. Marcus was initially confused by their reaction, as he was well liked around the office. Lachlan raised both hands in the air in an attempt to quiet the now hostile crowd.

'Come now, this is good news,' he said. 'Promoting internally creates a ladder and shows you can all move up if you work hard enough.'

'I thought I *was* working hard enough,' replied Tim.

'You told me I was in line for that promotion!' someone shouted from near the printer.

'Me too!' called Kevin.

Maree sat back in her chair. Lachlan had tried to motivate her with the same promise of promotion during her performance review. She was taken aback with the sudden mutinous nature of the sales group. Their chorus of voices became louder and louder as they all spoke over one other. Marcus looked around the room nervously.

'Please, settle down,' said Lachlan into his microphone. Maree could see his lips had started to quiver.

The employees became even more belligerent.

'You promised *me* that promotion!'

'Oh, this is such bullshit!'

'I've worked here longer than Marcus...'

'Please...' started Lachlan, as his hand began to shake. Marcus sat back down at his desk. More abuse was hurled at Lachlan until he became fed up and snapped.

'SHUT UP! SHUT UP ALL OF YOU!' yelled Lachlan.

The room was suddenly quiet.

'Of course I didn't *promise* you all the promotion. I dangled it as a possibility. I was trying to motivate you!' he said, pacing around outside his office. 'I told each of you that you were doing well and that if you kept it up the promotion would be yours. Marcus did the best. Therefore *HE* gets the promotion. Do you know how hard it is to motivate such a lousy miserable bunch? You're all so petty and useless. It's called WORK not FUN. I'm paying you to do your jobs not to watch videos on your phones!'

The staff shifted nervously.

'You suck!' someone called from the water cooler. Maree suspected it was Jane from Accounting.

'YOU suck! I'm sick of this!' said Lachlan, tossing his microphone down onto the carpet. 'Candice had the right idea about getting out of this place. At least she never has to see any of your worthless faces again!'

Lachlan pushed past the group as he headed for the door, loosening his tie as he went. For a moment no one knew what to do.

'Follow him,' said Tim. Everyone in the office scurried after Lachlan. Maree had become worried. Lachlan was clearly a man on the edge and there was no telling what he was about to do. Nobody in the office had ever seen him lose his temper. There was a feeling in the air that they were about to witness something special, something that they'd all talk about for years to come. Lachlan pushed open the main doors and threw his tie onto the concrete below. He was still fuming with rage. He stepped towards the portal outside their building and stopped in front of it, to address his employees one last time.

'Go on! Do it you wuss!' shouted a man at the back of the group.

'I hate ALL of you,' said Lachlan matter-of-factly. This statement resulted in an odd cheer from the crowd, as they realised what he was about to do. 'Good luck managing this lot Marcus! They are a disappointing bunch.'

Marcus didn't say a word, but looked terrified. He'd only just been promoted to second in command. Marcus was overwhelmed that he might suddenly be thrust into the role of manager. Maree turned her attention to Lachlan, hoping reason would prevail.

'Lachlan please don't do this,' she said.

'No, I'm done with the lot of you. Go to hell!' said Lachlan as he flipped everyone the bird. He turned on the spot and raised his hands triumphantly. Lachlan had always been so composed. The suit wearing, gel using company man had been the picture of professionalism. He now appeared to have lost his mind. Lachlan let out a huge breath as he faced the portal.

'I'm coming Candice!' he called as he started walking forward.

Before Lachlan could walk through the portal a bird swooped past him and vanished across to the other side. Inexplicably the green vortex closed in on itself, shrinking to nothing in an instant, and was gone. The group were shocked. Seemingly the bird flying into it had caused its closure. This was the first time anyone had seen a portal close. Lachlan was unable to move. Tim, Kevin and some of the other sales members started laughing at Lachlan before heading back inside. Maree felt sorry for him.

'Are you okay?' she asked.

'It… it closed,' replied Lachlan.

'Yeah.'

'Then she's really gone for good.'

Maree recognised Lachlan must have been harbouring strong feelings for Candice. Realising that there was nothing she could say she walked past Marcus and went back inside.

CHAPTER FIFTEEN

'As unpredictably as they arrived and without any clue as to why they came in the first place the portals are closing in on themselves,' said the reporter on the screen. Her name was Whitney Primrose and she was a well-known American journalist that frequently reported on worldwide news events. 'The event might seem random although some have noted that the portals seem to be closing after something is sent through them…'

The graphics at the bottom of the screen were abruptly changed to say *Breaking News*.

'Alright… I've just been handed this breaking news out of Europe. We've just been informed that two brothers in France are claiming to have returned through a portal,' said Whitney Primrose, looking a little flustered with this new development. 'That's right… these are unconfirmed reports at this stage. We will endeavour to bring you more information as it comes to hand. Early reports from our European correspondents suggest that the brothers… who are yet to be identified… jumped into a portal in Mexico and found themselves in Paris, France. This has experts speculating as to whether the portals are in fact a means of teleportation. The brothers are currently undergoing a physical evaluation.'

***

Maree opened Leon's computer at the dinner table. As she did, Val and Bill shot a confused look at one another. They were halfway through their meals but their daughter had not touched hers. She'd been too busy explaining Leon's complex novel to them to consume anything. When they'd continued to look at her blankly, Maree decided to go and get the laptop.

'I can't believe I hassled Leon about it so much,' she said. 'Now that I've read it, I want to know what happens next. It's so beautifully written too. I didn't know Leon had this kind of depth.'

'Neither did I,' mused Val. 'How about you Bill?'

'I didn't know he had any depth at all.'

'It's so sad. It's never going to be finished,' said Maree. 'And now the portals are closing.'

'Well maybe you could finish it?' offered Bill.

'I'm not a writer,' replied Maree, shooting Bill a look.

'Neither was Leon,' he replied.

'But he was! That's the thing… I think it's *amazing*!' Maree lit up as she scrolled through the document on the screen.

'And he wrote about you?' asked Val.

'A little, just at the start. I mean, my character dies pretty early on but without my death the main character doesn't push himself to discover the infinite capabilities of the human mind.'

Val and Bill looked at one another. They were confused with Maree's interpretation.

'He killed you off?' asked Bill.

'He had to. It inspires the whole hero's journey,' stated Maree.

'He killed off a character named Maree?'

'Yeah.'

'That doesn't sound very nice,' her mother said.

'You'll have to read it. I'm… *it's* a very important part.'

'So, your husband, who could write about anything, wrote a novel about your death and his rise to power. Have I got that right?' asked Bill.

'Well he becomes more powerful afterwards… yes,' replied Maree, considering the question. 'More or less.'

'So… he's better off without you?' continued Bill.

'In a way. The character that's based on me is sort of holding him back.'

'And do you think Leon felt that way about your marriage?' asked Val.

'No, of course not.'

'Okay…'

'He didn't!' protested Maree.

'Alright love. Eat your meatloaf,' prompted Val. Maree took a tiny bite of her food and chewed it until it dissolved.

'Maybe I should write a book,' said Bill.

***

It had started with a text message from Marcus. Maree didn't want to be at home with her parents. They'd been so dismissive of Leon's book that she'd become annoyed and retreated to her room to be alone. As she'd laid there on her bed Maree had wondered why they couldn't appreciate his work. This story was like his legacy. It was all she had left. As Maree was considering how she might begin to finish Leon's manuscript her phone had buzzed to life.

Do you want to do something tonight?

Maree had asked Marcus to meet her next door, at Greg and Vanessa's place. Now that she was back in their graffiti-soaked living room she'd questioned whether it was a good idea and had sent Marcus to search every room just to make certain they were alone.

'There's no one here,' he announced as he walked back into the living area.

'You're sure?'

'I've checked every room. We're alone,' he confirmed.

Maree had taken a broom to the carpeted floor and hurriedly pushed all of the mess to one side. They sat down on the three-seater sofa together, leaving the middle cushion between them as a buffer.

'I've been thinking about Lachlan,' said Maree. 'He was actually going to throw himself into that portal.'

'Yeah…'

'When I told him Candice was thinking about doing that he said it was a stupid idea.' Maree couldn't understand Lachlan's mental state, but knew Leon had probably felt the same way before he'd left.

'I guess the boss hates it here more than we know,' reasoned Marcus.

'What do you think is on the other side?'

'That's such a big question,' he replied.

'Come on…' urged Maree.

'I don't know, and I don't really want to know. There's nothing over there for me.'

'I've had no idea what I'm doing with myself lately. Leon left me... Candice left me. I feel so alone.'

'That's their loss,' said Marcus. 'And besides... you still have your parents... and me.'

'My father left us when I was ten years old. Bill is my step-dad.' Maree didn't usually share this fact with people but she felt like she was getting closer to Marcus, and thought he should know. Maree didn't usually like to qualify her relationship with Bill to others. He'd stepped up to fill the role of her father so naturally and seamlessly that she didn't want anyone to think he was less involved or less important for not being her biological father.

'Oh... okay.'

'For a long time I was sure that my father George had left because he didn't want to be a father. Then I realised it was because he didn't want to be married to my mother,' said Maree.

'She seemed alright to me.'

'Oh, she's fine these days. Mum and Bill don't argue because he's house trained. Bill cooks and cleans.'

'And your father didn't?' asked Marcus.

'I guess not. I can't remember everything but the thing that has stayed with me is the way my Mum used to nag my Dad. And one day he'd had enough and just took off.'

'Wow.'

'And you never saw George again?'

'Never.'

Maree picked up the cushion that sat between them and held it to her chest, crossing her arms around it.

'I've always thought Mum could have done more, you know? That she didn't try hard enough… or do enough to stay together.'

'Marriages aren't easy,' said Marcus.

'No… but you shouldn't just give up.'

'From the sounds of things neither of them wanted to work it out. I mean… your father left. So, how was she meant to try any harder?' asked Marcus. 'He'd bailed.'

'I don't know. I wish I could remember it more clearly that's all,' said Maree with a sigh.

I'm sure she did her best,' said Marcus as he shifted closer to her.

'Maybe. You know I used to be so careful about the guys I dated. I never wanted to have the same kind of relationship that she and George had. And I never saw any of the guys I dated as husband material.'

'So how did you end up with Leon?' he asked.

'He tricked me.'

Marcus looked surprised by this response.

'What do you mean?'

'He acted like the man of my dreams. He seemed perfect. When we were together almost a year we went on holidays to Los Angeles and he proposed and wanted to get married in Vegas,' said Maree, a faraway look in her eyes.

'And you did?'

'Of course I did,' replied Maree. 'I was so naïve and stupid. I wanted to believe that he was different. For a while it felt right.

And then he lost his job and gradually I lost my husband. He couldn't pretend anymore I suppose.'

Maree realised that she had started to cry and wiped away her tears as quickly as she could.

'You are the architect of your life Maree. Leon left you, the same way your father left your mother, but then she moved on. Now she's happy with Bill. You'll be happy again too.'

Marcus moved himself to the middle of the sofa and boldly kissed Maree. She placed her hands on either side of his face and kissed him back. With each touch the moment intensified a little more until Maree wasn't feeling upset anymore. She sat up straight and threw her leg over Marcus, perching herself in his lap. He kissed her again.

'We don't have to do anything you don't want to do,' he said, in between kisses.

'That's great...' she replied, 'but I want to.'

Somewhere in the distance a car alarm was going off. Maree lay quietly on the sofa, waiting patiently for someone to turn it off. When the noise finally ceased, she felt uneasy. She'd made good use of Greg and Vanessa's place, playing house with Marcus, but she was still trespassing. Maree was also feeling strange about committing adultery, even though she assumed that her marriage was over. The way she'd left things with Leon still felt unfinished and open-ended. Maree stood up and started getting dressed. She could feel Marcus staring at her naked body, which made her feel excited. Maree liked the attention.

'I should go home,' she said.

'Me too.' Marcus picked up his clothes.

They both got dressed and he located his car keys.

'I had a good time,' said Maree.

'I hope you sleep well,' he offered.

'I think I will,' she replied with a smile. She leaned over and kissed him again. Being affectionate with Marcus was becoming second nature now.

Maree walked out the front door and into the cloudless night. Marcus followed closely behind.

'I'll see you tomorrow at work.'

'Okay.'

Maree watched him drive away. Suddenly she felt lighter and less self-destructive, as if everything might work out for the best. As she walked towards her house she spotted Bill's trailer reversing towards their garage. She froze and hid behind a nearby tree.

Maree wondered what he was doing, as it was now very late. She noticed that his trailer was full to the brim with furniture and unmarked boxes. Maree watched suspiciously as Bill checked the street and then closed the garage door behind him. She waited until Bill finished making noise in the garage before investigating his haul for herself.

***

'Mum, I have to tell you something.'

Maree shook her mother, who had fallen asleep in her comfortable living room chair.

'Why are you up? It's late,' said Val as she came to.

'I just saw Bill arrive home with a trailer full of stuff,' announced Maree.

'Oh… yeah?'

'It's other people's stuff! I think he's been breaking into houses at night,' she said.

'Yes, I know,' replied Val as she rubbed her eyes.

'What? You knew about this?' Maree was shocked that this secretive and illegal behaviour was being sanctioned by her mother.

'Yes.'

'And you're okay with this?'

'Look if other people want to jump through portals that's their business,' said Val. 'They can't take it all with them and we're retired Maree! We have to look out for ourselves.'

'But you can't just loot other people's houses!' cried Maree.

'Why not? They'll never know.'

'It's not right.'

'Your friend Candice started a trend. The people that leave aren't coming back. It's finders' keepers now,' said Val matter-of-factly. 'If we don't take it, someone else will.'

'I can't believe this.'

Maree was now looking at her mother with fresh eyes. It was becoming clear that Val and Bill were a unit, and that she existed just outside their bubble. They hadn't felt the need to include Maree on this venture, and had assumed correctly that she would be opposed to it.

'Relax,' offered Val. 'Bill told me about it days ago. Don't worry he's keeping an eye out for you too.'

'I don't want anything!' protested Maree.

'Well I told him to look anyway. In case we see something that you might like as a belated birthday present.'

***

Lachlan seemed smaller now. His office and its proportions now seemed to dwarf him, as he slumped in his chair. He looked defeated as Maree sat down opposite him. It had been hard to take him seriously around the office since his breakdown and Maree had noticed that defiance of his authority had recently become the norm. In front of her sat a box of expensive donuts.

'Thank you for making the time to see me,' said Lachlan.

'No problem at all.'

'Maree… I'm trying to speak to everyone in the office individually today and personally apologise. Oh, would you like a donut?'

'No thank you.'

'I'm seeing a psychiatrist now,' continued Lachlan. 'I haven't been asked to… I'm doing it because I have my own unresolved issues to work out. He and I agree that I had a momentary lapse of judgment.'

'We all have our moments. It's fine,' said Maree.

'Nevertheless, I shouldn't have taken my frustrations out on any of you and for that I'm very sorry.'

'I accept your apology.'

'Thank you Maree. You're the only one who understands what I'm going through.'

Maree suddenly felt herself become tense.

'How do you mean?'

'You've lost someone to these portals too,' said Lachlan.

'Um… yes.'

'Have you been missing Candice as much as I have?'

Maree was sure that he'd been talking about Leon and had not been looking forward to answering Lachlan's questions about her husband. She was able to relax a little knowing he was referring to Candice.

'I've been hoping she's happy. Wherever she is.'

'Did she ever talk about me?' asked Lachlan, sitting up in his chair.

'Sometimes.'

'Do you think if she hadn't jumped through the portal and I had… maybe… asked her out, Candice might have gone on a date with me?'

Lachlan had clearly been thinking about the night that Candice left, and the kiss that she'd planted on him before going. Maree decided that it couldn't hurt to give her manager hope, considering Candice had been unpredictable and constantly surprising.

'I think she might have,' she offered. Maree believed it too. Candice had dated across a spectrum, and never really had a type.

'Thank you. That means a lot,' said Lachlan with a smile.

'Did you see the reports about the brothers in France?' asked Maree. 'If the portals are used for teleportation that could mean Candice is somewhere out there.'

'Yes, I've been watching the news.' This surprised Maree, given Lachlan's previous stance on the portals and the misuse of company time. 'I'm concerned that she might have landed in the middle of the ocean,' he continued. 'Do you have any idea what Candice is like at swimming?'

'No clue.'

'Hmmm, it's unlikely that she's in the Western world or she would have called or emailed. Have you been checking your spam folder?' asked Lachlan.

'No, but I will.'

'Let me know if you hear anything?'

'Of course.'

***

Marcus was racing to catch up to Maree as she headed for her car. The day was over and they'd barely spoken, largely due to a training module that Marcus had been forced to attend. His promotion had also moved him into an office and out of Maree's line of sight.

'Hey wait up!' he called.

'Oh hey,' said Maree, car key in hand.

There was a gusty Melbourne wind that kept blowing her hair into her face, making her wish she'd remembered a hair tie.

'How are you doing?'

'Fine,' she replied with a shrug, tucking her brown hair behind her ear. She wondered why he didn't kiss her hello, and how he felt about their night together. Maree considered that perhaps their relationship had changed now that Marcus was technically her superior in the office.

'Did Lachlan apologise to you as well?' he asked.

'Sure did. So... do you get to keep your promotion?' asked Maree.

'Looks like it. Lachlan is on probation so if he does anything like that again you're looking at the new boss.'

Marcus smiled and adjusted his tie. Maree found the idea of promotion comical.

'Wow,' she said sarcastically.

'What?'

'You love this, don't you?' she said with a chuckle.

'Of course! I've been working hard for this promotion.'

'I've been working just as hard as you.'

Marcus screwed up his face.

'Don't be a sore loser about it,' he said.

'It's just a job. It's not that important,' said Maree defensively. His attack had left her reeling.

'Are you alright? Is this about last night?'

The way he spoke made Maree feel cheap and used. She didn't want to be the person he called late at night for sex.

'Don't worry about it. I just think I need a holiday,' she said dismissively. 'Did you see the brothers that teleported to France? That means Candice cou-'

'That was a prank,' interrupted Marcus. 'It's all over the news. The brothers were on holiday in France and they thought it would boost their prank channel on YouTube.'

'Really?' Maree felt deflated again.

'Yeah, they never went through any portal. They flew over from Mexico.'

'Oh. So... Candice...'

'She's probably not coming back.'

His words were so cutting and carefree. Marcus didn't care that people couldn't come back through the portals. He didn't mind that Candice was gone. Maree sighed.

'Hey, when are we going to go on that second date?' asked Marcus eagerly. 'I mean, last night was fun too but I'd like to take you out again.'

'Oh... I don't know.' Maree wasn't sure about Marcus. She'd wanted to move on from Leon but now her instinct was that she'd made a mistake. Marcus had said all the right things at the start but she was scared of diving into something new. After all, Leon had said all of the right things at the start too.

'I thought we had fun,' said Marcus, who looked suddenly confused.

'Yeah...' Maree shifted uncomfortably, passing her car keys from one hand to the other.

'I know you live with your parents and you probably don't want to keep breaking into your neighbours place so I was thinking this time maybe you could come over to mine,' offered Marcus.

'I think I have to say... no.'

'Why?'

'I feel like... the other night was maybe a mistake,' said Maree.

'No, it wasn't. That felt so right.'

'It wasn't right. I shouldn't have gone on a date with you in the first place. I shouldn't have slept with you last night. I still feel like a married woman. I can't start something up while I'm still married to Leon.'

'What changed?'

'I'm sorry. I didn't mean to lead you on.'

'So... you're *done*, just like that?' asked Marcus. He was clearly annoyed.

'I can't do this.'

'He's not coming back you know.'

'If I was ready to date anyone, it would be you.'

'Well that doesn't make me feel any better,' said Marcus.

'Well, I'm sorry. There's nothing I can do.'

'Do you know how many times I've wished for something like this?'

Maree looked perplexed.

'Do you know how hard it is to be in love with a married woman?' asked Marcus. 'How many days I wanted your husband to just disappear? Do you know how amazing it felt when you told me that he finally HAD?'

'It hasn't been so amazing for me,' said Maree.

'No, of course not. You can't stop talking about Leon,' said Marcus with venom in his voice. 'For me I thought this was going to be the beginning of *us*.'

'There is no us,' stated Maree.

'No. I suppose there never will be,' he replied.

'You're a nice guy Marcus. I know you'll find a nice girl who will love you, but I'm not her.'

'It's just too hard to get close to you with the elephant in the room. Enjoy being alone,' he said and walked away, shaking his head as he went.

CHAPTER SEVENTEEN

Maree hadn't watched her wedding video since they'd played it for Val and Bill. In retrospect her parent's reception to it had been frosty. Bill had been especially annoyed at the news that Maree and Leon had eloped in Las Vegas without them. Something about the rainy weather made her want to watch it now. Maree wanted to hear Leon's voice and see her husband's face again. She hated to admit how much she'd been missing him.

On the screen Leon was wearing a blue suit and top hat. The memory made Maree smile. It was one of the few times he'd dressed up for her. She saw herself wearing a rented wedding dress and beaming for the camera. It hadn't mattered that the rental place didn't have any veils available. Maree realised that she hadn't been that happy since. The two of them stood before an Elvis Presley impersonator as they said their vows. As her husband spoke, the Maree on the screen and the Maree watching the video both started to cry.

'I Leon, take thee Maree, to be my wedded wife, to have and to hold from this day forward, for better, for worse, for richer, for poorer, in sickness and in health, for as long as we both shall live.'

The Elvis impersonator made a grunting noise.

'Maree, repeat after me,' he said.

'I Maree, take thee Leon, to be my wedded wife, to have and to hold from this day forward, for better, for worse, for richer, for poorer, in sickness and in health, for as long as we both shall live.'

She watched herself repeat the words and bawled.

When she was done the Elvis said, 'Thank you very much.' It was the most he'd sounded like the King since the ceremony had started.

Leon laughed.

'I can't believe we're doing this!' said Maree as she stared into Leon's eyes.

'By the power vested in me by the state of Nevada, I now pronounce you husband and wife. You may kiss your bride,' said Elvis.

The camera zoomed in awkwardly as the couple in the video kissed. It felt like a lifetime ago for Maree. Some cheesy music played, and colourful confetti was thrown into the air. Most of it seemed to land in Maree's hair. She paused the video on a beautiful still frame of the two of them and collapsed onto her bed.

***

Bill was hunched over the dining table as he read the newspaper. Sometimes he would stop reading for hours and come back to it, making the event last all day. Val and Maree knew not to touch the paper if they saw it lying open, as Bill would inevitably return. Maree watched her mother doing a puzzle at the other end of the table. It was almost complete, the remaining pieces scattered before her. Her parents were so content in each other's company. Nothing about this silence was awkward.

'If you want to help me do the puzzle now I'm afraid I'm not after any help. You can't just swoop in at the end and get all the glory,' joked Val.

'I think you've got it from here Mum.'

'Nearly there.'

Maree walked over to the television in the living room and turned it on. A reporter was standing on an empty street.

'All over the world the green portals are closing as they reach capacity,' he said. 'Most portals have disappeared completely in densely populated areas as citizens are taking it upon themselves to fill the portals up with everyday items...'

Maree realised that she hadn't been paying attention to the news lately. It appeared that the world now knew how to get rid of the portals and were taking it upon themselves to remove their threat entirely. The world was returning to normal.

Maree looked out the window at the portal outside her house. The old woman from across the street was standing next to it, bathed in the green glow it provided. She was dressed in a woollen robe and was spraying water from her garden hose into the middle of the floating vortex. Maree's eyes went wide as she connected the dots.

'She's filling it up,' she mumbled to herself.

When that portal closed Maree would never see Leon again. She didn't want to give up on him. She was suddenly faced with a choice, and Maree knew what she had to do. She walked over to her parents.

'I've got to go out for a while,' she said, surprising herself with the announcement.

'What are you on about? It's the middle of the night!' exclaimed Val, removing her half-moon glasses and looking up from her puzzle.

'I can't be here right now.'

'Do you want me to come for a walk with you?' asked Bill.

'Thanks, but I'll be fine,' said Maree.

'Okay, try to take notice of which houses have no lights on. It could mean they've left,' said Bill.

'Sure…'

'Do you have to go out now?' asked Val.

'I think I should. Before it gets to be too late. Finish your puzzle Mum.'

'Alright.'

Maree was saying goodbye in her own way. She knew her parents would never approve of what she planned on doing next. She lingered behind her mother, taking a mental picture of everything she was leaving behind. Val systematically picked up and put down pieces.

'I could get you your own puzzle if you'd like?' offered Val, who had noticed Maree lingering.

'I don't think I'd ever finish it,' stated Maree.

'Well, I could always help you if you get stuck.'

Maree smiled sadly, knowing that her parents would miss her the most.

'Thanks Mum, you've helped me enough. You two are pretty great,' said Maree as she fought back tears.

'I know I am but don't give him a big head about it,' Val said, pointing at Bill.

'Too late Val! I knew I was the best!' laughed Bill. 'Don't forget Maree, houses with no lights on, alright?'

Maree smiled and nodded.

'I'm really glad you two have each other,' she said.

'Take a coat, would you? It might be cold out there,' said Val, motioning towards the coat rack.

'Thanks Mum.'

Maree took her wedding ring out of the handbag that she'd hidden it in. She slid it onto her finger, grabbed a yellow cardigan and walked out the front door.

***

'Wait! Stop!' called Maree. Her cries startled their aging neighbour. Instinctively she turned her hose to the ground as Maree approached. The old woman looked confused but said nothing. This staple of the community represented one possible future for Maree. If she stayed here waiting for Leon to come back to her, she might never take any chances. The years would pass her by until one day she wouldn't recognise herself. Maree considered that life was for living. Candice had taken the leap. Even her husband had dared to discover what was on the other side of these portals. Maree steadied herself and, much to the surprise of her neighbour, took a great leap into the unknown.

CHAPTER EIGHTEEN

It was insanely bright at first, but the journey had taken only a moment. Maree squinted as she got her bearings. The room was white from top to bottom and very vast like an empty warehouse. As her eyes adjusted, she could make out dozens of people and objects around her. Maree looked up and saw that the room went off in all directions endlessly. There was no obvious light source above her, but it reminded Maree of the fluorescent lighting in the sales office. Everything around her was illuminated, perhaps a little too harshly.

As Maree stood up, she tripped on a drone near her feet. She looked around and saw dozens of books, rocks, bicycles and assorted items that she'd assumed people had thrown through the portals. This seemed to be where everything had ended up. She scanned the nearby faces for Leon or Candice, but they were nowhere to be seen. Maree was startled by a bird that flew past her head. She was disorientated and confused. Maree wondered where she now was. The people around her were sitting indifferently. Some on manmade objects like cushions or mattresses but most seemed content to occupy the white floor below them. There were people deep in the distance too, none of who seemed to care that she had just arrived.

Maree walked ahead, passing a car that must have driven through a portal at some point. It was empty and undamaged, and Maree couldn't tell if the driver had intended this to be its ultimate destination. There were so many random animals scurrying around. The artificial light seemed to be confusing them. Maree eventually came across two familiar faces.

'Vanessa, Greg?'

Maree was astounded to see her neighbours in this strange new environment.

'Maree! Oh God. You jumped through too?' asked Greg, even though that seemed obvious. He was now sporting a very masculine beard.

'Where are we?' asked Maree.

'Nobody knows,' replied Vanessa. 'Most people think we're on an alien ship.'

'You mean you've been in this room the whole time?'

'Yeah. It's like a zoo. They drop us food and the lights go off intermittently to simulate night.' Vanessa shrugged as if it was now normal to her.

'It's horrible,' said Greg.

'Yeah, it's horrible,' agreed Vanessa quickly.

'Have you seen Leon?' asked Maree.

'Yeah he's somewhere around. He's been keeping to himself mostly.'

'I have to find him.'

She said goodbye to the couple and pressed on. The scene that unfolded before her was surreal. The people that sat around were like caged animals. They'd given up hope. Maree's searching eyes finally landed on her husband. Leon looked weary. He'd taken the furniture that he'd cleared out of the spare room and put together a small fortified area for himself. Maree smiled at the makeshift home he'd created. She wished she hadn't been so hard on him. Perhaps his decision to send their furniture through the portal had been a good choice after all.

'Leon!'

She watched her husband as his mouth fell open.

'Maree? Is that you?' he called, unable to believe his eyes.

Leon stood up from the two-seater sofa and walked towards her. They hugged for a long time without words. Maree was so happy to see him, and slightly less pleased to smell him.

'Are you alright?' she asked when the embrace finally ended.

'No. This has been a nightmare.'

'Is Candice here?' she asked. Maree was dying to hear that her friend was alright.

'No. There must be a different holding cell like this for each portal. Everyone and everything here went through the portal on our street. She's somewhere else,' stated Leon.

'So… you haven't seen her?'

'No!' he said, suddenly becoming aggressive. 'And we can't exactly leave!'

'We're trapped…'

'Yeah. I've been waiting here the whole time,' he said. 'What took you so long?'

This question annoyed her. Instead of answering it she decided to confront her husband.

'Why did you leave me like that? How could you?' asked Maree.

'I don't know. I wanted to hurt you.'

'Well… you did.'

'Mission accomplished then,' said Leon. 'Why did you finally come through after me?'

'I had to see you again.'

'You thought you could save me, huh? Well, it's too late, isn't it? Now we're trapped together.' Leon was being unnecessarily hostile. It had started to annoy Maree.

'You never should have jumped through the portal in the first place,' she said.

'None of us should have! We all thought we were *so* important. We thought that the portals would lead to a better place. Look how wrong we were.'

Maree looked around at the vast expanse of nothingness. It felt like they were in limbo.

'The portals were like a net that these aliens draped over the Earth,' said Leon dramatically. 'They caught us all. They didn't even have to coax us into jumping in. We're supposed to be the most intelligent life forms on the planet. We were dumb. We walked into the portals like animals. We did this to ourselves.'

'I wish you'd listened to me,' said Maree.

'I wish you'd say anything worth hearing.' Leon's tone shocked Maree.

'Is this how it's going to be with you from now on?' she asked.

'Maybe.'

'Yeah? Well I don't like it. I don't like the way you've been treating me,' said Maree.

'I made a mistake, okay?' Leon sat back down on the sofa and crossed his arms. The sparse amount of furniture arranged before her made Maree think that they were in a play. The scene felt inauthentic and incomplete.

'I read your book.'

'What?' he was startled by this news. 'I told you, it wasn't finished.'

'I liked it. Even though you killed me off.'

'I had to. It's the inciting incident that starts the whole journey,' said Leon.

'I know why you did it.'

'You do?'

'I do.'

'Is that why you came after me? To tell me how much you liked the book?' asked Leon.

'I guess I jumped through after you because I wanted to face my problems head on. The way my father George never did.' Maree had used many of her birthday cake wishes as a teenager hoping that her father would return to her.

'And I'm your problem, am I?'

It was clear that Leon had not changed. He had piled up the familiar wreckage of their past life and stewed in it, remaining the same way he had been before. Maree looked at the rounded glass dressing table that used to be in her parents' spare room. The mirror was now cracked. She sighed to herself and realised that her relationship with Leon had not been perfect. She had forgiven every flaw after he'd abandoned her, building Leon and the memory of their marriage up in her mind. Looking at the garbage around her made Maree see that the emotional baggage of their relationship had followed them here, in the same way the furniture had. Chasing Leon might have been a mistake, but she was now ready to face the consequences of that choice.

'I want a divorce.' Maree walked away from Leon and the remains of their life together on Earth.

CHAPTER NINETEEN

Maree couldn't sleep. The lights on board the alleged alien craft were too bright when they were on, and she'd found the duration that they were off to be too short to enjoy a blissful sleep. When she closed her eyes, Maree tried to imagine the exterior of the vessel that she was now apparently inside. Everyone kept saying that aliens were to blame. She didn't know what to think. This new environment was like being in a quiet void. It didn't feel like they were moving and she couldn't be sure that they'd even left the Earth's surface. Maree had considered that their captors might be torturing them all, depriving them of essential sleep in order to break their will. But why were they feeding them if they were also torturing them? Food and water was being provided in bulk. It dropped into the room via a series of light blue portals that never appeared in the same place twice. At first people had tried to leap through the food portals in the hope that they could escape this cage, but it proved impossible. The daily appearance of the blue portals was a random event.

Maree had taken up residence near Vanessa and Greg, making them her neighbours here as well as back home. Her ex Leon had hassled her every day after Maree had ended their relationship, and she'd become unwilling to discuss anything with him anymore. If they were to be trapped together for the rest of their lives in this place at least she could untangle herself from him. Leon had disappointed her too many times and Maree couldn't ignore it. She'd felt a weight come off her shoulders after proclaiming her desire for a divorce. Even though it wouldn't be possible to legally separate from Leon, due to their unknown physical location, she'd moved her wedding ring onto her necklace as a symbolic gesture. She didn't want to dispose of the ring completely, but she couldn't quite pinpoint why.

'Did you want to eat with us?' asked Vanessa.

Maree nodded politely and joined them in their area. There was a smattering of useless objects from Earth including a broken television set that had been arranged in an attempt to normalise the scene. Vanessa had gathered a pile of food and water and was about to share it with Greg. The rations that their unseen overlords provided were all compacted into indistinguishable cubes, while the water was delivered in small orb portions with a dissolvable layer around them. The food seemed nutritious but lacked any real flavour. The consistency reminded Maree of dog food. The orbs of water would only dissolve when they were consumed, and made contact with the tongue. The way the food and drink were packaged and distributed here made Maree think they were inside some kind of insane experiment. She'd wondered why they had been left here, and why nobody had told them anything. It had bothered Maree at first, but she'd become used to it, just like everyone around her. The human race seemed very adaptable, no matter the environment. Maree thought this place was quite hospitable really. The only thing that was annoying her was the absence of hygiene. She was dying to shower and brush her teeth and it had only been a week.

The most curious thing about the space they now inhabited was that the temperature was always perfect. This led some of the residents of the white void that they occupied to shed their clothing. There was no system of law and order and without anyone regulating the behaviour of the people they did whatever they felt like. The only action that seemed to be enforced was dealing with excrement. Everyone performed the same march away into the distance where an area had been designated as a communal bathroom. It was isolated enough that it didn't smell but it was definitely a challenging place to walk towards when nature called. People had loving dubbed it Crap Town. Maree liked staying near Vanessa and Greg for security. Some of the men had assaulted a woman two nights earlier and she was on edge because of it.

Greg passed a handful of food cubes to Maree and she hungrily devoured them. She was thankful that the food was delivered in large quantities and that at least nobody was fighting over it.

'So... you were saying that the portals had started closing?' prompted Vanessa.

'Yeah. They were filling up... reaching capacity. People were throwing things into them until they closed,' replied Maree.

This information had become the currency that she exchanged for their friendship and protection. Vanessa and Greg were desperate to hear as much news from Earth as possible in the hope that they might find a way home. Maree had also told them as many stories as she could remember, movies she'd seen and things she'd read online. She didn't tell them that she'd broken into their home, stolen back her *American Beauty* DVD and had sex with Marcus on their sofa. Maree also neglected to mention that their lovely home had been ransacked and vandalised. Her neighbours were always riveted, watching her as she spoke. In this place stories were all they had.

'How's it going with Leon? Has he been bothering you at all?' asked Greg.

'No. I asked him to respect me and stay away.'

Leon had pushed his sofa closer and now lived about sixty metres away from them. He seemed to understand not to come any closer. It was like an unspoken restraining order had been filed against him. Maree had seen Leon watching her from afar but always pretended not to. She could see he was hurt and annoyed by the break-up. Leon had taken to having his meals at the same time as Maree. It was like having a stalker that she couldn't do anything about, except ignore.

'Do you think it's weird that we haven't seen any aliens?' asked Maree, changing the subject.

'What do you mean?' Greg had ingested a cube and now spoke with his mouth full.

'Well like… who's in charge here?'

'No idea.' Vanessa shrugged.

'So, who's feeding us?' asked Maree. 'And why?'

'Why are they *feeding* us? Because otherwise we'd die…' reasoned Greg.

'So, they clearly know we're here. And they haven't told us why we're here… or even where here is. And instead of answers we get food cubes.'

'I like food cubes,' said Greg, devouring another.

'Could be worse,' stated Vanessa. 'At least we weren't incinerated. That's what I was most afraid of.'

'Then why did you jump through?' asked Maree. It had been bothering her that they'd said goodbye to Leon but not to her.

'I didn't want to miss out,' said Greg. 'I figured we were living this half-life… we had this horrible mortgage. Why not change everything all at once? And when Vanessa agreed we didn't hesitate.'

'I always thought you two were so happy,' said Maree.

'We're happy with each other, sure. But you need more than a happy relationship. The world gets in the way. You have to work and pay back the bank and you just get drained…'

'We couldn't have a baby,' blurted out Vanessa.

'Oh… I'm sorry. I didn't know,' replied Maree.

'We tried. And we saw specialists and had all the tests. It's my fault. I'm not hospitable enough…' Vanessa spoke with a straight face. She might have cried about this in the past, but she appeared to be done with that now. They'd accepted the fact that they couldn't conceive.

'We didn't have anything to lose, I guess,' said Greg.

'Well I'm glad you're here. You've both been so nice to me. I really appreciate it,' said Maree.

'Did you and Leon want to have kids?' asked Vanessa.

'Well… we never really figured it out, I guess. I've always wanted to… I mean… I figured that was the next step for us,' said Maree. She caught a glimpse of Leon as he peered at them from his sofa. 'But now I'm kind of glad we didn't. It makes it easier to end things between us.'

Vanessa looked a little sad as they all chewed their food in silence.

***

The lights were abruptly turned off to create another artificial night. It was never announced, and the lights were never dimmed, so Maree always found the event to be a shock. She faced away from Greg and Vanessa as they'd proceeded to have noisy intercourse with one another in the dark. It was uncomfortable for Maree and she pretended to ignore it as she stared out into nothingness. After a short time her eyes had adjusted to the low light. When her neighbours were finished they both found sleep much more easily than Maree. She could see figures moving around in the distance. She wasn't comfortable using her yellow cardigan as a pillow. Maree didn't feel safe.

***

When the simulated morning lights turned on a woman's shrill screams woke most of the occupants in the room. Maree sat up and headed towards the cries. She was one of the first people to arrive and the scene was disturbing. A man had been stabbed to death with a screwdriver. It was too violent to have been self-inflicted. The murder weapon was still wedged in the man's neck, just beneath his beard. The culprit would be impossible to identify.

'Oh my Lord… Aaron's dead… he's dead…' the nearby woman said over and over again.

'Who did this?' The question came from Leon. He'd pushed through the handful of sticky-beaks and climbed onto a chair. Leon scanned the crowd, a scowl on his face. The group were silent.

'This isn't right!' he yelled.

The woman had stopped wailing and she was now stroking Aaron's forehead. Maree had never met the deceased man. He didn't look familiar.

'You're animals!' the woman sobbed.

Everyone remained quiet and then slowly dispersed. Whoever killed Aaron seemed certain to get away with it. With no central authority the society was doomed to devolve into chaos. Maree hoped that this behaviour would not be repeated but worried that it was inevitable. They were all trapped in the same hell, and everyone had their breaking point.

As Maree tried to walk back to Vanessa and Greg a hand clutched her, holding her arm tightly.

'I need to talk,' said Leon.

'I don't have anything more to say,' replied Maree. She shook herself free of his grasp and went back to her friends. She told Vanessa and Greg about the murder, and while they weren't as shocked as Maree had been, their lovemaking seemed more furious that night.

CHAPTER TWENTY

Maree woke up with a hand covering her mouth. Her eyes were wild with fear as she struggled in the darkness against her attacker.

'Maree, it's me…'

She recognised the voice. It was Leon.

'Don't make a noise. I'm going to take my hand off your mouth. Please… don't wake up Vanessa and Greg.'

Maree stopped struggling and Leon removed his hand.

'Jesus… you scared me. I thought I was being murdered,' she whispered.

'I'm sorry. I wouldn't have done this unless it was completely necessary.'

'What do you want? I told you I've got nothing to say to you.'

'It's not about that. Maree… I know a way out of here.'

She squinted to get a better look at his face. He looked earnest.

'What are you talking about?'

'I know what's going on. If you trust me… and come with me now, we can get out of here,' pressed Leon.

'What about Vanessa and Greg?'

'They can't come.'

'Why not?'

'It's got to be just the two of us. This is important.'

'Why?'

'Listen Maree, do you want to stay here?' whispered Leon angrily. 'Please...'

'Leon...'

'I can't leave you here. Not with a murderer on the loose.'

'Are you messing with me?' she demanded. 'This isn't funny.'

'It's not a joke. You'll have to trust me.'

Maree decided to give him the benefit of the doubt. Leon seemed to have her best interests in mind, even though he was prepared to leave Vanessa and Greg behind.

'Okay. I'll come with you,' said Maree as she collected her cardigan and stood up.

They walked carefully away from everyone and into the distance. Leon was leading them towards Crap Town.

'Where are we going?' she asked.

'As far away as possible. I don't want to cause a riot.'

'Why would we cause a riot?'

'Because of this.' Leon revealed a small black box. It was not clear what it was or how he'd acquired it. Soon they were adjacent to Crap Town, at a safe distance from everyone.

'What I'm about to show you will be a lot to comprehend all at once. Just take a deep breath and trust me, okay?'

Maree nodded and did as he instructed.

'I love you,' said Leon.

Before Maree could answer or object he pressed the black box. A stream of orange light poured forward and a bright swirling portal appeared in front of them.

'How did you…' Maree's voice trailed away.

'Trust me, okay? Just go with it,' repeated Leon. He held out his hand and led Maree into the orange portal.

***

Their journey was almost instantaneous. As soon as they'd walked through to the other side the portal closed behind them. They found themselves in a new environment now, with dark marble-like blocks on the walls. The room was about five metres wide and had clearly defined dimensions and decent lighting, unlike the holding room they'd just escaped from. This new space also smelt a lot better than Crap Town.

'Where are we?' asked Maree.

'We're in some kind of meeting room,' replied Leon.

'Who are we meeting?'

'Our hosts.'

Maree stared at her ex-husband. She wondered how it was possible that this man, out of all the people in that room, had devised an escape. She felt grateful, but extremely confused.

'How do you know *any* of this?' she asked.

'I've been in this room before. I've met one of them.' Leon scratched his growing beard. It suited him more than she cared to admit.

'When?'

'Yesterday.'

A wall at the opposite end of the meeting room changed colour and another orange portal appeared. They were no longer alone in the room. The creature that teleported in to join Leon and Maree was like nothing she'd ever seen. It was a light grey coloured blob that slid into the room with the body of an oversized slug. Its torso was made up of seven long arms, like a malformed octopus, each one split at the tip like the claws of a lobster. The alien's face consisted of two large dark eyes that sat towards the top of its grey elongated body. Maree covered her mouth in shock.

'Don't be afraid,' said Leon. 'It's just saying hello.'

The being made no sound but continued its approach. Maree clenched her fists, not knowing how to react. The creature stopped in front of her and stretched out one of its arms.

'Do I… *shake*?' Maree looked to Leon for cues.

'Let it come to you,' he advised.

It slid forward and slowly moved one of its limbs out in front of it. Its approaching arm looked a little bit like a long grey tongue, forked at the end. It eased towards Maree's chin. She stayed as still as possible, as though the being was a dog, sniffing her to make sure she was not a threat. The arm rose and gently touched Maree on the forehead.

The creature made an instant psychic connection with Maree, filling her head with knowledge and imagery. She inhaled, feeling suddenly overwhelmed with the exchange. Maree collapsed backwards and Leon caught her in his arms. She felt dizzy but managed to sit up.

'I…'

'It's okay,' said Leon. 'It happened to me too.'

'What was that?' asked Maree.

'I think it's the way these aliens communicate. They told me things… *showed* me things and gave me a mission.'

'Me too…'

'Maree, do you know about the portals now?'

She thought for a moment and found that she now knew all about them. Her mind was racing with knowledge.

'Yes,' she replied.

The alien had informed Maree that the Earth was dying. Their planet was approximately two hundred and nineteen years from complete extinction. The aliens were peaceful in nature and had entered the Earth's atmosphere with the long-term goal of saving the human race, as they had done with countless other civilisations. The portals were intricately planted and left on a timer. They were supposed to activate in one hundred and ninety years but an archaeological dig in Greece inadvertently triggered the portals prematurely. Once the sequence had started and the portals had opened all over the world the aliens had to take immediate measures to make sure any life forms that came through would be saved. Their initial plan was to deposit a device on a new planet known as K-non, with a similar atmosphere to Earth. When people evacuated the Earth in the future they would be instantly delivered to their new home. The alien ship was currently en route to K-non, but wouldn't reach their destination for three days. When the portals had opened on Earth everything that was sent through had landed here, and not on K-non. The saviours of the human race had never intended on housing so many humans on board their transportation vessel but had been forced to improvise as they were still in transit.

Maree blinked hard. They *were* on an alien spaceship. Suddenly she knew why they were all being held in that room. They weren't supposed to jump through the portals – not yet. The aliens weren't ready for them. The device hadn't been set up on K-non. It felt strange to know these things with such certainty. The green grid around the Earth shouldn't have been activated in their lifetime.

'It's a lot… I know,' said Leon as he watched her processing this new information.

'It's just… so good to have the answers,' said Maree, feeling tears forming in her eyes. 'They wanted to save us.'

'Yeah.'

The creature was still loitering in front of Maree. It's dark eyes remained expressionless and it slid backwards to the far wall.

'Why did they tell you? Couldn't they have told *all* of us?' Maree was still feeling bad for the people who were left in the dark. She hadn't forgotten that there was a killer in their midst either.

'They opened a portal near Crap Town and I was just the closest person,' said Leon. 'I walked through and met this creature. He touched me and told me what was going on.'

Maree searched her mind for more answers. She now knew the origins of the portals and realised that this creature had tasked Leon with a mission. He had been asked to return to Earth and tell the population the truth about K-non. Now that the process had commenced, the aliens were planning on re-opening the grid of portals around the world and inviting the human race to join them on their new planet. Nobody would be forced to come, but those who wanted to would be welcomed.

'They asked *you* to do this…' said Maree.

'Yes.'

'So why am I here?'

'Because I wouldn't leave you behind,' said Leon. 'I told them I would only deliver the message if you came back with me.'

'To Earth?'

'I can't leave you behind in this place.'

Maree was filled with affection for Leon. He'd finally considered her feelings and she couldn't help but hug him.

'Thank you,' she managed to say.

'That's ok. So, you'll come with me? I think it's waiting for an answer,' said Leon as he indicated towards the alien in the corner.

'Of course I will.'

With her acceptance verbalised the creature re-opened an orange portal and vanished. Maree turned her attention back to Leon.

'What about everyone else on board? What about Vanessa and Greg?'

'We can't bring everyone with us. Even though they don't know it they're on their way to K-non now. They'll all arrive in three days and the portals will re-open on Earth.'

Maree nodded. Vanessa and Greg would be fine for three more days. She would have to focus. Their new mission was too important to ignore.

'The portals… when they re-open on Earth… it will only be for a two-hour window,' said Maree, understanding that this information had been deposited into her mind by the creature.

'That's right.'

'Will that be enough time for everyone on Earth to evacuate?'

'Not everyone will want to come,' replied Leon nonchalantly.

'But we have to convince them to. The Earth is dying, remember?'

'You let me worry about that, okay?'

'Ok Leon. When do we go back?''

'Now. If you're ready?'

'I guess I am…'

Maree didn't want to be on this alien spaceship anymore. Leon took the black device from his pocket. He held it out in front of him and clicked the top of it. A large red portal opened against the wall of the room. Maree put on her yellow cardigan and turned to her ex-husband.

'It's red,' observed Maree.

'Yeah.'

'Is it safe?'

'As safe as any of the others I'm sure.' Leon stepped closer to the portal, which swirled slowly and reminded her of lava.

'And this will take us back to Earth?' she asked.

'That's what they communicated to me.'

'Are you ready?'

'Let's go,' said Leon with a smile.

Maree took a deep breath and side-by-side they walked into portal.

CHAPTER TWENTY-ONE

As always the journey took only a moment. Maree was thrilled to see a bustling cityscape on the other side. It was home. The portal had opened on a concrete path and Maree and Leon found themselves surrounded by spectators. Many of the people around them were filming them with their phones and yelling. It took a moment for Maree to get her bearings. The environment, while definitely Earth, was unfamiliar to her. Leon waved at the cameras and addressed the crowd.

'Hello everyone. My name is Leon and this is my wife Maree.'

She didn't say anything, as she wasn't about to qualify their relationship status to this group of strangers. Maree noticed the Space Needle in the distance and realised they had landed in Seattle. When she and Leon had eloped, they'd only travelled from Los Angeles to Las Vegas. She'd never ventured anywhere else in the United States, as Leon hadn't wanted to rent a car. Maree had always wanted to fly further East to New York or Washington, and had always regretted it. While Seattle was still on the West Coast, she was happy to be somewhere new and exciting. She was glad they hadn't landed in the ocean and wondered whether their destination was prearranged or pure luck.

'Listen to me,' continued Leon. 'We've come back through the portals. You've just watched us… this isn't a hoax.'

The crowd before them started to murmur. More phones were pulled out. The eyes of the world were now upon them. Maree felt underdressed.

'We've got a message for you all. My wife and I will be holding a press conference tonight.'

Maree screwed up her face.

'A press conference?' she asked Leon.

'Yeah… we need as many eyeballs as possible,' he replied in a hushed voice.

'Can you confirm the existence of aliens?' one man yelled out.

'Yes.' Leon replied in a deliberately vague way.

'Where did all the portals go?' a woman called out.

Suddenly the questions were coming from all around them. Leon lifted his hands to silence the crowd, but the noise only intensified. From above them a helicopter appeared. It made its descent and the people were forced to scatter. Leon and Maree held each other as several men in flak jackets grabbed them and dragged them on board. Neither of them resisted. Before they knew it, they'd been whisked away by these mysterious men. Maree could see that they were still being filmed as the helicopter lifted into the air.

***

'Once again our top story today concerns the mysterious red portal that opened in downtown Seattle this afternoon. Eyewitness reports have confirmed that a married couple, believed to be from Australia, have returned to Earth via this portal. If this proves accurate, this couple would be the first to ever return from the other side. This is a truly unprecedented occasion that some have compared to the moon landing in regard to historical significance. The male returnee made a speech to onlookers where he stated that this was "not a hoax" and allegedly confirmed the existence of aliens. We have been told that a press conference will be held tonight. Channel Four will bring you more details as they come to hand…'

***

Maree had been separated from Leon as soon as they'd landed. The noise from the helicopter blades had made it impossible for them to communicate but he'd smiled and nodded at her, as if their capture was all part of the plan. She considered that the aliens might have communicated more information to Leon, so she tried to be optimistic. Maree was now sitting alone in an interrogation room. She didn't like being held against her will. Her experience aboard the alien ship had changed her perception of freedom, and she was disappointed to have escaped their prison only to find herself in a fresh one.

Maree had no sense of time as she waited in the room. She thought about Leon and hoped that he was alright. After what felt like about an hour she was joined by an older woman wearing scrubs, rubber gloves and a protective mask around her mouth. Maree straightened herself up, having realised she was slouching.

'Hello ma'am,' said the woman, whose hair was tied up in a black and grey bun. Her voice was raspy, and seasoned with time.

'Hi,' replied Maree, who felt too young to be referred to as a ma'am.

'I'm a registered nurse. Tell me how you are feeling?'

Maree considered the question. 'Trapped,' she replied.

'Trapped?'

'Yes. I was trapped after I went through the portal and now I'm trapped here again.'

'Well we don't mean to make you feel that way. The Government here in the United States of America has recently passed some laws about the portals you see.'

'Oh…'

'The portals have been deemed a threat by the President, and so they are treated as such. We're to seize anything that travels through a portal… you understand?'

'But we're Australians… we're from Earth,' stated Maree.

'Well now, who's to say? When those kids from the Internet said they came back through the portals they were snapped up by European officials too. They were searched and prodded and pricked until they confessed that it was all a lie,' the nurse said with a grin. Maree felt nervous. She knew about Guantanamo Bay and thought she sensed a sinister undertone to the nurse's statements.

'Where is my husband?' she demanded. 'Is Leon alright?' Maree felt like they were still a team, even though she'd expressed her desire to get divorced. *Nobody else knows about that, she thought. What happens in space stays in space.*

'Leon is in a holding pen just like this one. He's been checked for biochemical agents and now he's being interviewed. Leon is fine.'

'And you're here to check me?'

'Yes.'

Maree consented to the required swabs and tests, feeling as though she had little choice in the matter. She was disappointed to discover that there was a mandatory cavity search but she allowed that too.

'You seem perfectly healthy to me,' the nurse said, removing her rubber gloves. 'How far along are you?'

'I'm sorry?'

'You're pregnant, aren't you?' asked the nurse.

'No…'

'You didn't know? Alright, have a seat.' Maree had been standing and re-dressing herself. She slumped into her chair.

'I'm… pregnant?'

'Yes.'

'Oh…'

Maree *had* been feeling tired, but she'd assumed that it was because she'd been having trouble sleeping on board the alien craft. The nurse produced a pregnancy test and allowed Maree to take it into the bathroom. It confirmed her suspicions.

'Now honey, there hasn't been any documented evidence about pregnancy in terms of exposure to portals… it might be like radiation…'

Maree had stopped listening to this woman's lecture. Her mind was racing. She hadn't had sex with her husband in a long time. Maree was worrying about how she was going to tell Leon that he wasn't the father.

'When can I see Leon?'

Maree had submitted to a lie detector test and two interrogations from men that she assumed were Secret Service agents. In front of her now was a non-descript man in a white shirt and black suit. He wore his sunglasses throughout the interview, and reminded her of one of the *Men in Black* as he kept pressing her for alien secrets. She wondered whether she'd have her memory wiped with a neuralyzer like in the film.

'You'll be reunited with your husband for the press conference tomorrow.'

'Tomorrow?'

'Yes.'

'Can't I see him tonight? I really need to talk to him.'

'I'll see what I can do,' he said as he left the room.

Following the initial tests they'd moved Maree to a special quarantined area with a comfortable bed. She now had a television, although it wasn't working. The most important new addition to her situation was the shower. Maree took a thirty-minute shower as she tried to wash the memory of the alien ship away. She tried to forget the smell of Crap Town and the ordeal she had endured. The faces of Vanessa and Greg kept flashing into her mind, and she prayed they would arrive safely at K-non soon. Maree considered what kind of planet K-non would be. She assumed that the aliens would choose a place similar to Earth, but perhaps it would be superior. She wondered whether their new home would contain other settlers, or whether there was a native population. Maree smiled to herself, knowing that Vanessa, Greg and Candice would prefer their new home to their current situation.

She was pleased to find an assortment of new clothes had been purchased for her and that her American hosts were now supplying a surplus of food. Maree gobbled down a chicken burger, mashed potatoes and a fruit salad. She thought about her parents. Did Val and Bill see her on the news? If they'd seen a glimpse of her were they savvy enough to search for her on the Internet? Maree made a mental note to call them as soon as she could. She took a nap, hoping to be woken by her Leon's return.

***

'And how would you describe your mindset?' asked the psychiatrist.

'My mindset?' Maree wasn't sure what he was trying to learn about her. She didn't want to say the wrong thing.

'Do you have any negative thoughts? Do you mean to do any harm to yourself… or others?'

The psychiatrist seemed too frail to Maree. He looked like he should have retired many years ago but had been dragged in as a specialist for this occasion.

'I don't want to hurt myself. I just found out I'm pregnant,' replied Maree.

'Mazel tov!'

'Thanks.'

'Is your husband excited?'

'He doesn't know yet.'

'Well I will talk to the higher ups. Let's see if we can't get him in here tonight for you, yes?'

'Yes please. Thank you.'

Leon had promised the crowd a press conference. Maree was starting to get anxious about keeping that promise.

***

'What does this mean for us? If two people can come back through the portals does that mean we can expect everyone to come back? Your thoughts Monica?'

Monica Sanchez was a model. She wasn't used to getting hit with difficult questions. She held up her book *Friendship across Dimensions* as she spoke.

'Rick… like… I can't…'

'Sorry it's *Mick*,' said the interviewer.

'Right, Mick. I believe… like… that we will see a grid of red portals opening in the next few days. I think everyone will be coming back through the portals… including my bestie Candice.'

'And what makes you think that?'

'Well… like… they went when the portals were green… and they'll return when they're red. Green is for go and red is for stop.' The interviewer furrowed his brow. He'd been finding this interview with Monica to be a challenge.

'I have heard *worse* theories…' said Mick as he tried to regain his composure.

'Don't forget to buy my book *Friendship across Dimensions*, which is now available as an audiobook!'

***

Maree was pacing the room out of boredom. There were no windows, except for one that faced out into a corridor. She wondered what time it was and whether she'd be fed again soon. There were two guards that appeared intermittently to check on her. She'd brushed her teeth and was considering preparing for bed when the door opened, and Leon appeared. He'd shaved his beard off and looked much cleaner.

'Leon! Are you alright?' Maree threw her arms around him and hugged him tightly. By doing so she'd pinned his arms to his sides, meaning the gesture couldn't be returned even if he'd wanted to.

'I'm fine. How are you?'

'I was so worried. Did they ask you about the alien ship?' Maree was suddenly full of adrenaline.

'Yeah. We're going to have to give a statement about the portals tomorrow morning. It's all been arranged.'

Leon was so calm and even-tempered. Maree was impressed that he was handling everything so well.

'They've been holding us here all day,' she said. 'The portals are going to re-open in two days. Did you tell them?'

'Maree… I spoke to the President.'

'Of… the United States?'

'Yes.'

'And?' Maree was dumbfounded.

'I told him everything.'

'And what did he say?'

'He signed off on our press conference.'

'Wow.'

Leon sat down on the bed with Maree and placed his hand on her leg.

'You smell good,' he said.

'Thanks. The shower here was amazing. Maybe the best of my life,' she said with a smile.

'I had one before,' stated Leon.

'Why did they keep us apart?' she asked.

'They wanted to independently verify our stories. To make sure we weren't lying.'

'And now they know we're not, right?'

'Yeah. They believe us. There have been some attempts… pranks I think… people have been pretending to come back. We're the first. They have us on video coming back through a red portal,' said Leon. 'They had to be sure.'

'I did a lie detector test too,' said Maree.

'So, they know we're being truthful. Now we just have to do this press conference tomorrow.' Leon noticed the TV and pointed towards it. 'Have you turned this on?'

'It doesn't work,' said Maree.

Leon shrugged and lay down on the bed.

'It's late. We should get some sleep,' he said.

Maree lay down next to her husband. She wanted to tell him about the baby, but she felt scared. This child had been conceived after he'd abandoned her. Leon shifted his body to face her and she mirrored him.

'I wanted to say thank you Leon.'

'What for?'

'Not leaving me behind on the spaceship.'

Leon furrowed his brow at the statement. 'I would never leave you behind. You're my wife,' he said.

Maree smiled and kissed him on the lips. Leon hesitated at first but then tilted his head to accept it. The two made feverish love in the dark for the first time in a long time.

CHAPTER TWENTY-THREE

'Do you trust me?' asked Leon.

'Yes.'

Following their evening together Maree didn't hesitate to answer. She'd never had a better sleep than the one she experienced last night. Her husband had rescued her from a nightmare and brought her home. The Secret Service guards had assured them that after the press conference they'd be allowed to contact their families, and Maree couldn't wait. She'd left her parents without telling them where she was going, and she'd felt guilty about it ever since. She had imagined Val and Bill being worried, and maybe even reporting her disappearance.

'I'll take the lead if that's okay with you,' said Leon.

'That's fine.'

Maree hadn't considered what questions they'd be asked, only that the whole world would be watching. Leon had spoken to the President and presumably he'd been briefed on what to say.

'You look beautiful by the way.'

'Thanks.' Maree had enjoyed the care of a team of professional make-up artists that morning and looked better than she'd ever looked before. She'd never seen any of the products they'd applied to her face and assumed they were expensive and rare.

She could feel herself blushing. Leon gave her a kiss. She tried not to think about her pregnancy and was glad that she hadn't exhibited any signs of morning sickness yet. She'd been able to keep it a secret for now. Maree vowed to tell Leon when the time was right. She wanted to wait until after the press conference, when they had a moment alone.

They stepped through a dark curtain and paced towards the waiting media. Leon sat down first. When Maree saw how many cameras and microphones had been set up she was too nervous to move. The press conference had been limited to ten members of the press, but she thought even five would have seemed daunting.

'Come on…' Leon coaxed her over with a wave. Maree eventually made her way to a chair. Leon held her hand just beneath the table, out of view of the reporters.

A man in a suit that Maree had never seen before was acting as the moderator.

'Yesterday prior to your detainment by the US Government it has been alleged that you verified the existence of aliens?' said one reporter.

'Yes, that's right,' confirmed Leon.

'Can you describe these aliens for us?' called out one reporter.

'Tell us what they looked like!' demanded another.

Leon let go of Maree's hand and placed his hands out in front of him. She could feel her heartbeat quicken.

'After my wife and I went through the portals we found ourselves on board an alien ship. Initially we did not meet our captors, until right before we came back.'

Maree silently considered that his phrasing made it seem as though they had voluntarily jumped through to the other side together. Leon was revising history in order to keep their marital issues a secret.

'Could you describe the environment on board the ship for us, please?'

'The room they kept us in was white. It was very bright… too bright probably. Some people got headaches.' Leon shook his head. 'And from time to time the aliens would just kill the lights. We think they were attempting to simulate night time, but it was too dark.'

'Did they tell you that?'

'No.'

'When did the aliens speak to you?'

'As I said… we didn't meet them for some time. They left us there to rot,' said Leon. 'All we had around us were the items that had travelled through the portals. So, we didn't have beds or creature comforts. It was a big, mostly empty room.'

Suddenly all of the reporters started asking questions at once, causing the moderator to spring into action. He silenced the media representatives and restored order.

'Could you elaborate on the aliens themselves? What did they look like?' Maree could tell that the reporters were growing impatient. They demanded to know more about the aliens themselves. Leon shot Maree a look before continuing.

'The truth is… and this is the message we wanted to tell the entire world… the portals will reopen tomorrow evening.' Leon exhaled and paused. The reporters started to murmur amongst themselves.

'It's true-' said Maree, before she stopped herself. She was still nervous about speaking to this huge audience.

'The same grid of portals will re-open tomorrow night. The portals will appear in all the same places they were the first time,' stated Leon.

'Why? What do the aliens want with us?' asked a nervous looking man at the back of the group.

'The conditions on the alien ship were like prison. They fed us, and provided us with water... but we were prisoners all the same.' Leon's eyes changed and he slipped his hand beneath the table once more. He interlocked his fingers with Maree's.

'The portals are a trap.'

All of the reporters in the room started asking questions at once, speaking over each other desperately. Maree looked at Leon. She was confused. *Why was he saying that?* She wondered.

'You should stay away from the portals tomorrow night. If you go through you will be a prisoner in a human zoo! It's a miracle that my wife and I were able to return. We tackled an alien and stole his teleportation device. The grid of portals is a net and they aim to capture as many humans as possible this time. Stay away from the portals, I repeat, stay away if you know what's good for you!' commanded Leon.

The reporters all started flailing their arms wildly. It was overwhelming for Maree. She was stunned. She couldn't speak and couldn't comprehend why Leon was lying to everyone. The portals weren't a trap. The aliens were trying to save everyone. She'd seen it for herself when the alien had communicated it all to her. The Secret Service men descended on them both and whisked them out of the room. Maree watched as the reporter's faces turned, and they became unruly.

'There will be no more questions at this time,' said the moderator. 'Thank you.'

Leon and Maree were taken into another room and left alone.

'Why did you say that?' asked Maree. 'Why did you lie to everyone?'

'Maree… listen… when I spoke to the President yesterday, I told him that the portals were going to re-open. He told me that he considered the portals an invasion and that he was going to send a bunch of nukes through to the other side. I told him not to do that,' said Leon.

'Good. So, you told *him* the truth?'

'Yes. I told him that the Earth was dying and that the portals were the only way to escape. I told him about the aliens… and about K-non and everything I knew.'

'And he told you to lie?'

'Yes.'

'Why?'

'He said that the Government needed to be in charge of this information. He said that he didn't want eight billion people jumping through the portal and overpopulating the new planet.'

'But if they stay here, they'll die,' protested Maree.

'Not right away. The world ends in two hundred years. That's at least three or four generations from now.'

'What?'

'The President made some good points. There is no infrastructure over there. No system of government. Who would be in charge in the new world?'

'You're dooming everyone in the world to death.'

'So? If the portals didn't accidently activate then we'd all be blissfully ignorant anyway. It's not even going to happen in our lifetime Maree.'

'I can't believe this. You don't want to go through to the other side? What about Candice?'

'I'm not really thinking about Candice right now,' replied Leon.

'She's my friend,' said Maree. 'And she's been on some alien ship much longer than you and I were.'

'She'll be fine. Everyone that's already taken the leap will wind up on K-non and be saved anyway. They're on their way there. You know that…'

'Why didn't you tell me about this?'

'You never would have gone along with it,' stated Leon.

'I know. I would have done the right thing,' said Maree.

'Listen, I want you to stay with me. If we keep our mouths shut we're going to have a very good life together.'

'How would you know?'

'It's been arranged.'

Suddenly it was clear. Leon had made a deal with the President. The leader of the free world would probably use the reappearance of the portals for his own selfish gain. Knowing when and where the portals would reappear was like a license to dispose of any people or problems you wanted to. Leon had been compromised.

'I don't think I can go along with this,' she confessed.

'You have to. If you don't play along, they won't let you talk to your parents. You need to do as I say Maree, okay?'

'I...'

'This is important. And the alternative is isolation. Do you want to be thrown in another holding cell?'

'No.'

'So, you're in?'

Maree didn't want to cause problems. She wanted to talk to her parents, and so she agreed to comply. 'Fine.'

'Good,' he said. Leon forced Maree into a kiss. She let him, but knew that things had changed between them. She no longer wanted to tell him about the baby. Maree wasn't sure what to do anymore.

CHAPTER TWENTY-FOUR

'My fellow Americans… yesterday we were gifted with the information that we are not alone in the universe. We've suspected this for many years and can now put our suspicions to rest,' said the President, in his televised address to the nation. The two American flags behind him drooped limply towards the floor. 'We are preparing ourselves for a potential invasion with an unknowable force. The people of Earth could soon be inundated with alien wormholes for the second time this year. I must stress that you should stay away from the portals at all costs. From the moment they reappear our best people will be working out how to close them. We need to be prepared for whatever happens next. God bless the United States of America, and God bless the people of Earth…'

***

The first perk that Leon and Maree were enjoying was the comfort of a five-star hotel. They were still being guarded, but now their every wish was being accommodated. Leon had enjoyed a massage and had ordered a platter of seafood. The Presidential suite was very opulent, with golden fixtures in the bathrooms. The bed was so large that when they lay down at either end Leon and Maree could stretch their arms out and still not touch their fingers together.

Maree was waiting patiently for her lunch. Leon had forgotten her disdain for seafood, leading her to order a sandwich separately. Maree was still eager to call Val and Bill as soon as possible. Her minders had promised that a computer would be supplied for them soon. Maree thought they might be intentionally stalling. She wondered if there was something online that they didn't want her to see. She also wondered what Leon was keeping from her. Maree had started to feel ill. She couldn't tell if it was because of the pregnancy or due to the lie that they'd told the world. That lie now bound her to Leon, whether she liked it or not.

'So, guess what?' Leon wore a plush robe from the bathroom.

'What?'

'They're publishing my book.'

'Who is?'

'A publisher. They're rushing it into print to capitalise on our new fame,' replied Leon.

'Your book about the infinite capabilities of the human mind?' asked Maree.

'Yeah.'

'But it's not finished.'

'I know,' he said, 'but they're calling it Part One! I'm getting a huge advance to write the next part.'

'That's... great, I guess.'

'I've been talking to a publicist and he's arranged for us to do another interview... we're getting paid a ton for the exclusive too,' said Leon.

'Another interview?'

'Yeah... to promote the upcoming book. If you like I can get you a copy...'

'I've already read it, remember?' Maree was becoming agitated.

'Oh yeah... I forgot about that.'

***

Whitney Primrose was a popular American journalist that Maree was familiar with. She'd started her career as a court reporter before moving into politics. Whitney had become a talking head on morning television where her role was to 'dumb down' the real issues for the average potential voter. Her popularity in Middle America had led to a high-profile position on a primetime current affairs program, and a cushy gig interviewing celebrities. Leon and Maree were seated on a plush sofa opposite Whitney in their Presidential suite. Her team of cameramen and stylists had decorated half of the room in preparation for this interview. Maree had been reluctant at first, but since sitting down they had delivered on their promise of a laptop. After they spoke to Whitney, and continued to comply with the President's agenda, she'd be free to call her parents. It was that simple.

'So, let's talk about this book,' started Whitney. She'd addressed the question to Leon but was watching Maree closely.

'Absolutely. It's a science fiction novel about the infinite capabilities of the human mind,' replied Leon.

'Sounds fascinating. Was it inspired by your journey into the unknown?'

'I'd actually written the book prior to our adventure together. I'm so happy that there's an interest in it now.' Leon spoke as though he were a seasoned writer, ignoring the fact that nobody had heard of him before now. Maree knew that the only reason a publisher was interested in his novel was because they were the first people to ever return from the other side.

'Let's talk about that adventure, shall we?' continued Whitney. 'If I can ask you Maree, were you scared aboard the alien vessel?'

'I was…'

'Tell me more about that.'

'Well, we were left alone. Nobody knew what was going on. People weren't sure what to do,' replied Maree.

'It was chaos. People had started to become violent,' said Leon, taking over. 'I'm glad I was there to protect my wife.'

'Did you witness this violence Maree?' Whitney was clearly trying to include Maree in the interview.

'Yes. Some people couldn't handle being locked up and left alone like that. I didn't feel safe.'

'Let's talk about the escape. I know I'm dying to hear about your heroics Leon. Tell us about that.'

'Well... I woke my wife up. I told Maree that I couldn't leave her behind. I wanted to make a run for it.'

'And how could you escape? You mentioned it was a sealed room?'

'It was. They were delivering us food from time to time. They'd drop it in using a series of portals. These aliens are so technologically advanced... like you wouldn't believe. Like... the ship was temperature controlled too. Anyway, I noticed that the food portals were appearing in a set pattern. I used that pattern to escape.'

'Incredible,' said Whitney.

'After I'd convinced Maree to come with me, I waited right next to the place where the portal was going to appear. And when it did, we jumped through.'

Whitney looked at Maree, causing her to nod in agreement. She was committed to the lie now.

'Did you need much convincing?' Whitney asked Maree. 'It sounds like you wanted to get out of there.'

'I did,' said Maree. 'It didn't take much convincing, no.'

'So, when you jumped through the food portal... what did you see?'

'The food portal... which was blue by the way... led us to a room. In that room was an alien creature. I guess his job was to feed us,' Leon said, seemingly inventing these details on the spot.

'And what did it look like?'

'He was slimy. He looked like a huge slug,' stated Leon. 'He had lots of arms. You wouldn't want to mess with him.'

'Leon, you keep addressing it as a *he*. Would you say it was a male?'

'I have no idea. There was no way to tell.' Leon was on a roll, while Maree remained silent.

'So, *it* had the body type... or consistency... of a slug?' asked Whitney.

'Yes.'

'Was it slow moving?'

'That's the thing,' said Leon, 'it wasn't. I got the impression he was a threat. Like it was a creature to be feared.'

'Were you afraid of it Maree?' asked Whitney.

'Yes... it was grey and...' she looked at Leon. He nodded for her to go on. 'It had long arms like an octopus.'

'And did it speak to you?' asked Whitney.

Leon cleared his throat, signalling that he would take over once again.

'It… came towards us,' said Maree, not understanding her husband's desire to respond.

'It looked like it was about to attack,' interjected Leon. 'So, I started to kick and punch… it's all a blur actually.'

'So, it never spoke to you?' the reporter asked. Maree could feel the camera's lens burning a hole in her. She was scared of being outed as a liar.

'No.'

'Then how do you know it's intentions? Perhaps you merely startled it,' offered Whitney.

'I can understand what you're getting at, but it was about to attack us,' said Leon.

Whitney Primrose pursed her lips suspiciously. 'But by your own admission you told me the creature was feeding you. Why was it feeding you if it intended to harm you?'

Maree felt herself starting to sweat. The lights seemed hotter than before and reminded her of being on the other side aboard the alien ship.

'You really had to be there,' said Leon quickly. 'We reacted the only way we could in that situation. If I hadn't fought that alien, then we wouldn't be here right now. Don't forget, Maree and I are the only people to ever return.'

'That's true,' stated Whitney.

'Well, when I hit the alien, he dropped a black device. It opened the red portal that transported us back to Earth… to Seattle…'

'It must have been a huge relief for you both.'

'It was,' said Maree.

'I for one can't wait to read the book,' stated Whitney. 'Even if it's not about the portals, I can see that you have quite an imagination.'

'Uh… thanks,' he replied.

'Just one more question Leon…'

'Yeah?'

'When you arrived in Seattle, and when you spoke at the press conference with your wife, you claimed that the portals would reopen in three days' time.'

'Right. That's tomorrow.'

'My question is, how did you know that? If you never interacted with the alien that you claim to have fought… if he never *spoke* to you… how did you come upon this knowledge?' Whitney raised a curious eyebrow.

'W-well… uh…' Leon stammered.

'It's just that it's inconsistent with what you've just said.'

'I know what I said.'

It was too overwhelming for Maree, who couldn't control her body any longer. Without warning she vomited to the side of the sofa.

'Oh Jesus!' exclaimed Leon.

'Are you alright?' asked Whitney.

'Yeah…'

'Are you ill?' the reporter asked.

'No, I'm…' Maree decided that this was as good a time as any to announce this news to her husband. 'I'm pregnant.' She looked at Leon for a reaction. He was silent.

'Congratulations,' said Whitney.

Leon didn't speak.

'And congratulations to you too Leon. This is your first baby together, is that right?'

The air was thick with nervous tension. The happy couple suddenly seemed anything but.

'Let's cut, shall we?' Whitney signalled to the crew and the interview was halted. 'That was great guys. Really good. So, we're just going to shoot a little more with you Leon, on the roof of the hotel. We've got a photographer up there and we need some images of you for our website.'

'Okay… great,' replied Leon. He seemed more than happy to leave the room.

'You don't mind waiting here do you Maree?' asked Whitney. 'We might need to get some B roll of you for later.'

'That's fine.'

Leon left the room, accompanied by Whitney and the crew. Maree had saved her husband from answering a difficult question by revealing her darkest secret. The ball was in his court now. Leon had become an excellent liar. Maree hoped that he'd be happy to lie about the baby too.

CHAPTER TWENTY-FIVE

Maree had just finished brushing her teeth when Whitney Primrose walked back into the Presidential suite. Maree was setting up the laptop with the intention of Skyping her parents. It was a surprise to see Whitney returning so soon and she stood up to face her.

'Hi Maree.'

'Hi.'

'So, are you really pregnant?' asked Whitney.

'I really am.'

'You know I've been doing this job for a long time. I know when I'm being lied to.'

'I'm pregnant… I'm not lying about that.'

'But you are lying about something, aren't you?'

Maree became silent.

'I used to be a court reporter,' said Whitney, 'I know a battered wife when I see one.'

'Leon doesn't hit me.'

'Maybe not. But there are other ways to be abusive.'

Whitney let the statement fester as she stared at Maree.

'I want you to tell me what really happened. I'm a journalist. I only want the truth,' she said.

'It's just that… I can't.'

'Why not?'

'It's complicated,' replied Maree.

'I'm sure it is. Well, if you'd like someone to talk to… I'd be happy to lend an ear. Here's my business card.'

Whitney handed Maree a plain white card and then slipped her a black Taser as well. She widened her eyes as she did so, asking Maree not to draw any attention to the exchange. Maree's heartbeat intensified, suddenly realising that the reporter suspected someone might be listening to their conversation.

'Thanks,' said Maree.

'I'm staying at the hotel too,' advised Whitney. 'If you'd like to talk, I'm available any time.'

'Okay.'

Whitney Primrose left the suite and Maree pocketed the Taser quickly. It occurred to her in that moment that the room was more than likely bugged and that their interactions were being monitored. Maree had been too distracted by everything to even consider it. Her stomach churned and she ran to the toilet to throw up.

***

The familiar Skype ringtone made Maree smile. She'd had to wait until three in the afternoon to call Val and Bill. It was nine in the morning in Melbourne and her mother had been advised to be standing by. Maree was finally going to see her parents again. Leon had not returned from the photo shoot, but she didn't care.

The call was answered by Bill, who was too close to the camera.

'There she is!' he said with a laugh.

'Hi Dad! It's so good to see you. Is Mum there?' asked Maree.

'She's just bringing her toast over… Val? It's Maree!'

The computer on their end was repositioned and Maree was finally face to face with her parents. She was overcome by emotion.

'It's so great to see you!' she said.

'Hi love,' said Val.

'How are you both?'

'Fine thanks. How are you liking Seattle?' asked Bill. Val took a bite of her toast.

'I haven't really seen any of it. We're just… we can't go anywhere yet.'

'How's Leon?' asked Val.

'He's doing okay,' replied Maree.

'I'm surprised you got back together with him,' her mother stated.

'I didn't…' Maree trailed off.

'The papers have been calling you husband and wife,' chimed in Bill.

'It's complicated I guess,' said Maree.

Her parents had been briefed by the Secret Service in preparation of their Skype call, and seemed quite knowledgeable now.

'And we hear congratulations are in order,' said Val.

'For?'

'You're pregnant, aren't you?'

Maree's face flushed with embarrassment. She had assumed that Whitney Primrose would have left that part out of her story. Maree would have preferred to tell her parents herself, especially given that she was still in the first trimester.

'I am… yeah.'

'That's exciting,' said Bill.

'It's still really early,' said Maree.

'And is Leon excited?' asked Bill.

'I haven't really spoken to him… at *length* about it. He and I still need to talk.'

'Alright then.'

Maree took a deep breath.

'Mum?'

'Yes?'

'I wanted to apologise about the way I left,' said Maree. 'I should have told you.'

'It was very rude,' said Bill.

'I've been quite upset about it darling,' said Val.

'I knew you would be. It's just that… I needed to see my husband again. You understand, don't you? If Bill had gone through a portal you would have chased him…'

'Bill would never have left me.'

'It's true,' stated Bill.

'Alright… but I wanted to work at my marriage. I didn't want it all to have been a waste,' said Maree.

'It wasn't a waste. When I was married to George it wasn't a waste. I learned a lot from that time. And I learned what I didn't want,' said Val.

'I acted very impulsively. And I'm sorry I just left you,' repeated Maree.

'Do you know what I thought? When I'd worked out that you'd jumped through a portal?' asked Val.

'What?'

'I said you're too much like your father. George I mean, not Bill.'

'I'm sorry Mum. I shouldn't have done that.' Maree was now feeling emotional about the whole incident. She wished that she'd left a note or had the bravery to just say goodbye in the first place.

'I accept your apology. Don't worry about it anymore, alright?'

'Guys… when the portals appear tomorrow… you're going to steer clear of them, aren't you?' asked Maree.

'Yes of course. We'll ignore them just like last time,' said Bill.

'I love you two. It's so good to see you.'

'Love you Maree. Are you planning on coming home with Leon?' asked her mother.

'Eventually, yes. Leon's got this book release now and I suppose when all of this attention dies down we'll be able to sneak back into the country undetected.'

'Maree?'

'Yeah?'

'When you come back… I'll need you and Leon to get your own place.' Val had a serious look on her face.

'Why?'

'I told you that Leon wouldn't be welcome in my home. Don't you remember what he did to you?'

'But I've forgiven him…'

'You might have forgiven him, but we haven't. He's never apologised to me, or Bill.'

'But he's changed… we're having a baby for crying out loud,' protested Maree.

'I'll be more than happy to help you out with my grandchild, but I don't trust Leon. Frankly I don't think you should either. He's no good for you.'

'I can't believe you're saying this to me Mum.' Bill had wandered away. Difficult conversations were not his strong suit.

'I'm being honest with you because you're my only daughter. Sometimes people just don't belong together.'

'You're wrong.' Maree stared daggers at Val.

'There you go Maree, always defending Leon. I hope you're right. I only want you to be happy.'

***

When Maree had finished talking to Val and Bill her husband was still nowhere to be seen. He was keeping secrets from her, and her mother's words were now swirling around in her head, filling it with doubt. When Leon had spoken to the President, they'd hatched a plan together. They'd left Maree out of the loop, and time was passing quickly. Did Leon and the President have a plan for when the portals opened tomorrow? She'd been thinking about the Taser that Whitney had discreetly passed her. Maree wondered if she was in more danger than she thought. She'd been keeping the weapon close just in case she needed to use it in self-defence.

Maree hadn't told her parents that Marcus was the father of her unborn baby. There would be too many follow up questions, and she'd barely had time to process it herself. Maree wanted to see Marcus and realised that he'd probably be at work right now. She knew his email off by heart and sent him a message. He replied almost right away announcing his Skype username, and asking her to call. It wasn't long before his handsome face was smiling back at her on the screen.

'Well hello stranger,' he said.

'Hi Marcus. How have you been?'

'Well you know… work sucks. Lachlan has been pretty docile, so it feels like the energy has been sucked out of the room a bit.'

'Tell him I said hi.'

'You'll have to tell him yourself. Lachlan keeps saying we should fly out to the US to see you. He seems to think that if you've come back that Candice will too.'

'She's not with me,' said Maree.

'Can I tell you something?' he asked.

'What?'

'Lachlan's been talking about jumping through the portals when they reopen. He gave me a whole speech about how I'll have to step up when he's gone. I told him not to… I said he's going to wind up in a human zoo like your husband said… but Lachlan wants to see Candice again. He doesn't seem to see the risks. Did you see her when you were over there? On the other side?' asked Marcus.

'No. I never saw her.'

'Maybe I should tell him that… or maybe I should say that you *did* see her! And that Candice is dating some other guy. I don't know how else to talk him out of it.'

'Well, maybe you shouldn't,' offered Maree.

'I shouldn't?'

'Yeah. If he wants to go… let him.'

'But he'll be trapped. It's a trap… that's what Leon said.'

'Lots of places are traps. Lachlan probably thinks that office is a trap too,' said Maree.

Marcus studied her face through the screen.

'Is there something going on? Are you alright?'

'I'm fine. I probably shouldn't have called. I just… shouldn't be talking to you.'

'Why not?'

'Because we had an affair,' stated Maree.

'Your husband left you… it wasn't an affair,' he replied.

'I was still married.'

'I mean… *technically* you were…'

'I cheated on Leon with you. I shouldn't even be talking to you,' she said, as she shook her head.

'Then why did you call me?' he asked.

'I don't know.'

Marcus looked perplexed. The tone of the Skype call had changed. Maree shifted uncomfortably. She'd heard a noise in the distance, but it wasn't Leon. Nobody burst into the room to stop her.

'I saw your interview,' said Marcus.

'You did?'

'Yeah...'

Maree was conflicted. This was her opportunity to tell Marcus that he was the father of her child. Leon must have figured it out, which explained why he hadn't returned. Maybe he had run away again, instead of facing her. Maybe her parents were right. Maree considered whether she had anything to gain by telling the truth. She looked at Marcus but remained silent.

'Is it my baby?' he asked, seemingly reading her mind. His beautiful blue eyes were wide with anticipation. She hoped they were hereditary. Maree closed the lid of the laptop, terminating their call.

CHAPTER TWENTY-SIX

'And so, in conclusion, I believe that she's pregnant with an alien baby. One of these slug creatures that they described in the Whitney Primrose interview.'

'Why would they send her back then? If she's carrying their precious cargo?'

'It could be any number of things...'

'Such as?'

'The little one might be growing at an accelerated rate, standing by to pop out of her and go on a murderous rampage.'

'Has anyone confirmed her pregnancy, or are we meant to just take their unverified word on it?'

'She'll probably be sent straight to Area 51 so that she can give birth to the alien in a temperature-controlled room.'

'I mean... my question is; if the alien doesn't eat humans... what *does* it eat?'

***

Maree woke up and stretched. To her surprise her hand connected with Leon's shoulder. He must have returned while she'd slept. The portals were due to re-open that afternoon, and Maree was nervous. There were too many lies circling them, and too many things that remained unspoken. She decided to wake Leon up.

'Morning.'

He opened his eyes but didn't respond.

'I need to talk to you,' said Maree.

'You should have talked to me before we went on TV. How long have you known about the baby?'

'I only found out two days ago. When we arrived in Seattle.'

'And who is the father?' asked Leon.

Maree exhaled. She wasn't looking forward to the pain she was about to inflict.

'It's Marcus.'

'From your work?'

'Yeah…'

'That's the guy that you told me *not* to worry about? The one that gave you that birthday card? You've been sleeping with him?' asked Leon furiously.

'We were only together once. After you left.'

'Is that meant to make me feel better? That he impregnated you on the first try?'

'I wasn't *trying* to get pregnant at all!' yelled Maree.

'Well… you failed.'

'So… you don't want to be with me anymore?' she asked.

'You make me so mad Maree. Honestly… I don't know what you were thinking.'

'I wasn't thinking. But you were gone. I was scared… and Marcus and I just sort of… *happened*.'

'These things don't just happen. He's wanted you for a long time I'll bet. He was biding his time… waiting for his moment to strike.'

'It wasn't like that. We were just friends.' Maree tried to sound convincing and wasn't sure she'd pulled it off. She remembered Marcus professing his affection for her outside their office, and how happy he'd been when Leon went to the other side. Marcus had been patiently waiting for Leon to mess things up.

'I can't believe you cheated on me with the one person I confronted you about. Were you trying to hurt me?' asked Leon.

'Of course not.'

'And when were you going to tell me?'

'I don't know…'

'So, if you weren't pregnant you might *not* have told me?'

'You're making it seem like I'm some manipulative monster. I'm not. It wasn't like that,' said Maree.

'You cheated on me, didn't you? That's exactly what it's like,' replied Leon.

'You left!'

'So?'

'You abandoned me! I didn't think I would ever see you again,' said Maree.

'You weren't going to come after me?'

'At first I thought the idea of going through the portals was insane. First Candice… then you… I thought the world had gone mad.'

'You were just going to leave me there?'

'Leon, if I'd known then what I know now… I wouldn't have followed you. I regretted it as soon as I got there.'

'But I saved you. I brought you back with me.'

'I was only trapped on that spaceship *because* of you! It was your fault! You don't get credit for rescuing me from a situation that *you* put me in. If you pushed me in a well and then threw me a rope, I wouldn't be happy about it!' Maree was exasperated.

'So, what happens now?' asked Leon. 'You told me you wanted a divorce. And then you slept with me the other night... I feel like you're sending me mixed messages.'

Leon was right. She had to make a decision. She got out of the bed and started getting dressed. 'I don't think I can do this anymore,' said Maree.

'You don't want to be with me?'

'You're lying to the world about the portals. They're coming back tonight, and nobody is going to jump through them.'

'So what?'

'The aliens chose you for this mission and you're ignoring them. You're dooming the entire human race! Don't you see that?'

'The end of the world is two hundred years away! I've done the right thing by telling the American Government. They can spend the next hundred years figuring out how to make their own portals. We'll be long gone by then,' said Leon. 'We've got to enjoy this while we can.'

'I'm pregnant Leon. I want to have this child. That means that I have to think about the next generation too,' said Maree, pulling a jumper over her head.

'So, you're keeping that kid?'

'I was always keeping it.'

'We're done,' stated Leon. 'Marriage over.'

'I was afraid of that. I can't stay here with you,' said Maree, as she started to cry.

'Fine. Go ahead and leave if that's what you want. I won't try to stop you… but the guard on the other side of that door might.'

The portals were about three hours from opening. Maree felt for the Taser in her pocket and headed for the door. She furiously knocked to get the guards attention. He wandered over and let himself in.

'Oh, thank God,' said Maree, who was still in tears.

'What happened?' asked the guard.

'He hit me…' she said, pointing at Leon.

'What? Are you kidding me?' Leon was not amused.

'Is that true? Did you hit her?' the guard asked, turning his attention to Leon. He pushed the door open wider.

'No! I never touched her! She's a filthy lying whore!'

The guard took a cautious step towards Leon and in that moment, Maree took the Taser from her pocket and shocked the guard in the side of the neck.

'What the hell…' Leon jumped off the bed as the guard collapsed onto the end of it. 'Where did you get that?' he asked.

Maree didn't answer. She removed the handcuffs from the guard's belt and took a mobile phone from his pocket.

'Maree! What are you doing?' asked Leon.

'Handcuff yourself to the bed,' she demanded as she threw him the silver handcuffs.

'No!'

'Do it now Leon! I'll tase you if I have to.'

Leon looked into her eyes and saw that she was telling the truth. He put up his hands defensively.

'Okay Maree… look… I know there is a lot going on right now, but you can't act this way.'

'I can't sit by and let you decide what's best…' said Maree. 'The whole world should have a choice. *I* should have a choice!'

'What are you going to do?' asked Leon. 'You're still my wife.'

'No. A marriage is about compromise. You and I don't work. I can't be with someone who is so corrupt and selfish.'

Leon took a step toward her, and Maree held up the Taser.

'Don't even think about it,' she said. 'Not another step.'

'Can we discuss this? I think that-'

'No. That's enough talking. Handcuff yourself to the bed now. Last chance Leon.'

He reluctantly did as Maree asked, slipping the handcuffs through the metal bedhead. Leon was now positioned comfortably on the bed, with his hands above his head. The guard was still unconscious near his feet. Maree exhaled a sigh of relief.

'I can't stay here anymore. When the portals open… I'm going to the other side.'

'Maree! Listen to yourself. If we play ball, then we can have the good life here on Earth. You don't even know what it will be like over there.'

'It doesn't matter. Anything is better than staying here with you Leon. Goodbye.'

Maree took off her wedding ring and placed it on the bedside table. As she walked towards the door Leon started shouting for help. Maree took the Taser and blasted Leon in the chest, causing him to pass out. She took the guard's mobile phone out of her pocket and called the number on Whitney Primrose's business card.

'Whitney? It's Maree. I'm ready to talk, and you can have the exclusive… but it's got to be *now*.'

Maree watched the world go by through the window of the news van. She felt a tinge of sadness now that her plan had solidified. She was leaving this world having seen so little of it. Maree tried to enjoy the scenes as they zipped by. People drinking at a pub. A couple walking their dog. She was full of nerves.

'How are you feeling?' asked Whitney.

'I'm okay. I'll be better once we're further away.'

Maree had met Whitney Primrose and her cameraman in the lobby of the hotel. They'd escaped to the news van, which was parked nearby and left the hotel together without detection. The truth had spilled out of Maree. She'd told Whitney about the portals, the alien contact and that Leon wasn't the father of her baby. Maree had also agreed to film an exclusive interview for Whitney if they could do so in front of one of the portals. Rick the cameraman was driving the van. He still appeared to be in shock, having heard Maree's admissions firsthand. It was clear that they both believed her. Now it was up to Maree to make sure the world knew the truth. It didn't matter to her whether everyone on Earth jumped through the portals or not. She just needed to give them all of the information to allow them to choose for themselves.

'We're almost there,' said Rick.

'Good. Now Maree, we're going to be going live as soon as possible. My producer has promised me the feed will be nationwide. I'm just worried that it won't spread fast enough. Some countries are asleep right now and I don't-'

'It will have to be enough,' said Maree. 'It's all we can do.'

'And you're going to jump through?' asked Whitney.

'Absolutely. Are you?'

Whitney shook her head.

'I have a husband… a job I love. I've got to stay here and hope for the best.'

'I understand. Thank you… for everything.'

'Thank you, Maree. For telling the truth.'

***

They had selected the site of a well-known portal for their interview. Maree knew that all of the portals would open in exactly the same places as last time, but she had no local knowledge of Seattle. Whitney had suggested they all head to the International Fountain, a metal dome that blasted water into the air. The spot had been featured heavily on the news when the portals had first appeared, due to the fact that the Seattle Space Needle was visible in the background. It seemed perfect.

Maree was fitted with a lapel microphone and positioned in front of the Fountain, next to the place where the portal was due to appear. As Rick placed the camera onto his shoulder, Whitney called her producer.

'We're good to go,' she said after she'd hung up the phone.

Whitney and Rick both had earpieces in, and Maree nervously stood in front of the metal dome, waiting for the interview to begin.

'Thanks Tom,' said Whitney, suddenly shifting into her on-air persona. 'I'm standing here at the International Fountain reporting live with my very special guest Maree Allen. Hello Maree.'

'Hi Whitney. Thank you for having me.'

'We've been talking off air about your last press conference and your husbands warning regarding the portals. I understand you'd like to clear up some of the facts?'

'That's right,' replied Maree, steadying herself and facing the camera. 'My husband lied to you all. The portals are not dangerous. They are not a trap.'

'Your husband Leon stressed to the media that these portals… should they re-open… will lead us into a human zoo. Care to comment on that?'

'They *will* be re-opening. I can promise you that. We're not far away now,' said Maree. 'The truth is that my husband and I did *not* escape by fighting an alien. The alien selected us. It sent us back with a message.'

'And what is that message?' asked Whitney.

'The Earth will be uninhabitable within the next two hundred years. The alien race that sent the portals had intended that they be a means of escape when the end of the world is upon us.'

'So why did the portals appear at all?'

'They were activated prematurely. It was an accident. Some people, such as myself, went through and ended up on an alien ship. That part is true. But they weren't expecting the portals to open yet. The aliens weren't ready for us.'

'And this time they will be ready for us?'

'Yes. When the portals reopen here today that will be the signal that the aliens are ready for us,' said Maree, getting back on track. 'The portals will open on a new planet called K-non… that's where they will lead. This new place is similar in atmosphere to Earth and was selected by the aliens as a new home for the human race.'

'And what is your message to the people of Earth?' asked Whitney.

'First of all, I'm truly sorry for letting my husband lie the way he did. I didn't know he was going to do that.' Maree looked to Whitney, who nodded profusely for her to continue. 'When the portals reappear, I will be jumping through. The world is still many years from ending and if you want to stay here on Earth you can. But for those of you that want a fresh start, a clean slate and to ensure the long-term survival of our species… I urge you to take the leap with me.'

'It's a lot to take in, and of course with such short notice many people will be conflicted about whether or not they should believe your story.'

'My husband lied to you before, and I deceived you all by omission. This is my attempt to make things right. I don't know if the portals will open again in two hundred years. This might be our only chance to escape this planet. If people choose to believe me… then you need to jump through the portals. Please…'

Maree stopped when a glowing green portal materialised beside her. Rick adjusted his framing to incorporate Maree and the portal. Whitney placed her hand over her earpiece as her producer spoke to her.

'Maree I'm being told that the portals are opening up again all over the world. Can you tell us how long they will remain open for?'

'If you want to be transported to K-non you will need to travel through a portal in the next two hours. After that they will close, and I don't know if they will ever re-open.'

A helicopter could be heard whirring in the distance. The authorities had become aware of their transmission and tracked them down.

'And Maree, I know you're Australian. Any messages to your family and friends back home?' asked Whitney.

Maree smiled half-heartedly, knowing that they would be asleep due to the time difference.

'Mum… Dad… I'm sorry I didn't say goodbye this time. I hope you'll forgive me. Please know that I'll be okay. Marcus… you asked me a question last night… and the answer is yes. But I think you knew that already…'

The helicopter was now almost directly above them. Maree started to step towards the portal. She could hear Whitney hurriedly trying to wrap up the live cross as men in bulletproof jackets descended from the helicopter via ropes. Maree smiled at Whitney, eternally grateful to her for allowing this moment to happen. She offered the camera a peace sign, in the same way Candice had done, and threw herself dramatically backwards into the portal.

CHAPTER TWENTY-EIGHT

The first thing Maree felt was calm. The helicopter had been whipping up the wind around her and the pursuing government officials had been loud. Now that Maree had landed in a completely foreign environment everything was still and peaceful.

Her first impressions of the planet K-non were positive. The world seemed flat and green. There were large tropical trees, many of which appeared to bear fruit. There was a thick tree line that looked like it could be optimised for shade and shelter. She could see a familiar grid of portals stretching out into the distance, but nobody was coming through after her. Maree was feeling disheartened until she saw the alien creature.

It might have been the same one that sent Leon and Maree on their initial mission but she couldn't be sure. It slithered towards her with slow but deliberate movements.

'I did as you asked,' said Maree as it approached. 'I did my best.'

The creature extended its long grey arm and touched Maree on the cheek. In that instant the alien transferred another package of information to her. Maree saw in her mind's eye the interview she'd completed with Whitney Primrose spreading throughout the world. Everywhere on Earth people were talking about and considering whether they should jump through a portal. Her message had gone viral.

'It worked… they know the truth,' she exclaimed happily.

The alien had communicated its gratitude for her efforts. The communication exchange was overwhelming. In that instant she knew that the aliens would continue to aid in the development of the planet K-non, providing it with food and infrastructure, until it was self-sufficient.

'Thank you,' said Maree. 'But I'm the only one here…'

The alien reached out and touched Maree on the stomach, this time flooding her with images from the future. The scenes that Maree was privy to involved her daughter. Maree could not believe it. She was shown a vision of K-non that was now thriving, where she lived in a completed town with her daughter. Seeing her own blue-eyed offspring, a child that she didn't even know about a few days prior, was incredible. Maree wept with joy. She now knew that everything was going to be okay. It was an incredible gift.

A number of small blue portals opened nearby, and a delivery of rations were dropped onto the soft surface of K-non. She recognised the orbs of water and the cubes of food from her time on the spaceship.

'But it's just me,' she protested. 'That's too much food for-'

A yell interrupted her. And then another could be heard in the distance. Suddenly there were hundreds of people arriving through the emerald portals. Maree covered her mouth with both hands. She saw people from every race converging on the new planet. Maree walked over, prepared to welcome them to K-non.

***

She'd been nervous about the new arrivals at first. The portals had remained open for two hours as specified, and it had been a nerve-wracking time for Maree. She estimated that there were twenty thousand people gathered around her now, but knew that there would have been multiple drop zones on K-non. There was no sign of Leon, although he could have easily hidden amongst the arrivals. Maree was worried at first that her husband would pursue her in an attempt to continue to control her. After the portals closed her intuition told her that he hadn't, instead choosing to live his new life as a single celebrity author. He'd have to field questions now that Maree had outed him as a liar. She suspected that those who'd elected to stay probably didn't believe her anyway. It didn't matter now. She knew her parents were still on Earth too. They were set in their ways and were happily enjoying their twilight years. They had already experienced a lifetime full of adventure. Maree knew that they would be alright as long as they were together. She thought about the President, and whether he would have sent anyone through. It didn't matter if he had, as on K-non everyone was equal.

The alien had made itself scarce as people had started arriving, but the aliens' influence continued. In the days that followed the people of Earth became used to their new home and appreciative for the ongoing delivery of sustenance. Soon it just felt like they were camping in a place where the temperature was perfect.

***

On her fifth day on K-non Maree heard a voice calling out to her from beyond the tree line near her shelter.

'Maree!'

It felt impossible but here on the other side of the galaxy her friend had found her.

'Candice?' Maree jolted upright.

The two hadn't seen each other since Candice had bravely opted to throw herself through a portal all those weeks ago. So much had changed but Candice still exuded the same beautiful spirit as she always had. She ran over to Maree and the two hugged and laughed.

'Hey you.'

Maree was so glad to see her friend as that meant that everyone on the spaceship had landed somewhere on K-non. Vanessa, Greg and everyone that felt trapped and forgotten would now have answers as well as a new home.

'Nice to see you Maree,' came a second familiar voice.

It was Lachlan. He looked so informal against this new expanse. He looked happy.

'Lachlan? You jumped through too?'

'Of course. I knew if there was even the slightest chance that it would lead me to Candice then I had to do it. And of course, I trust your word Maree.'

Candice walked over to Lachlan and kissed him on the lips. It was a surprise to Maree that they had paired up so quickly.

'I see it's worked out for the best then,' said Maree happily.

'Sure has,' replied Candice. Her friend was beaming with joy.

'I've got so much to tell you,' started Maree.

'There'll be time for all that. But first...' Candice pointed past Maree, prompting her to turn around. Standing before her was Marcus, who had tears in his eyes.

'He jumped through with me,' said Lachlan.

'And after they'd found me, we all decided to find you,' added Candice.

Maree's mouth fell open and she walked towards Marcus. She threw her arms around him and they cried together.

'I hope those are tears of joy?' asked Marcus.

'Definitely.'

'You were right Maree. About what matters the most...'

'It's your baby,' confessed Maree. She'd wanted to tell him sooner.

'I know,' he replied. 'I saw you on TV. I've missed you so much.'

'I've missed you too.'

'I know I told you that I would never jump through the portals,' said Marcus.

'You said there was nothing over there for you,' replied Maree.

'Well this time there was,' he placed a hand on her stomach. 'I'm here now, if you'll give me another chance?' pleaded Marcus.

'Is that your question of the day?' she replied with a chuckle.

He smiled and held her in his arms. Everything felt immediately right. She was so happy that they'd all found each other again.

Maree was now truly ready to start again. Everyone would have a second chance here on K-non. She was filled with hope for the next generation, and for her daughter. She'd tried to offer the human race another choice, an escape from the world they'd known. Some had embraced it, while others had chosen to go down with the ship. Maree considered that the people who'd elected to stay had probably doubted her words. It didn't matter anymore. The population had fractured, and they were on a new path now.

Maree stared out at the lush green land in front of them. Marcus held her tightly and kissed her. Everything about that moment felt right.

'It's beautiful, isn't it?' Marcus took a deep breath as he stared into the distance.

'If you like green,' replied Maree with a smile.

'Oh, I do.'

'Me too.'

THE END

About the Author

David Farrell lives in Melbourne with his wife and children.

He has Directed two independent feature films and has a film

Podcast called *Pod Me If You Can*.

His stories *The Last Resort, The Glove* and *Dropping the Belt* are available now as e-books and on paperback. Check out his short story compilations *Twelve & Twelve More*, which are also available as audiobooks.

You can contact him @DaveFarrell1 on Twitter